MISS MATCH

MISS MATCH

BY SEBASTIAN ROBERTS

"Success is building the person
you are happy to die as."

TATE PUBLISHING
AND ENTERPRISES, LLC

Published by Tate Publishing & Enterprises, LLC
127 E. Trade Center Terrace | Mustang, Oklahoma 73064 USA
1.888.361.9473 | www.tatepublishing.com

Tate Publishing is committed to excellence in the publishing industry. The company reflects the philosophy established by the founders, based on Psalm 68:11,
"The Lord gave the word and great was the company of those who published it."

Book design copyright © 2015 by Tate Publishing, LLC. All rights reserved.
Cover Art by Thomas R. Cuba
Cover design by Niño Carlo Suico
Interior design by Gram Telen

Published in the United States of America

ISBN: 978-1-63449-126-6
1. Fiction / Contemporary Women
2. Fiction / Romance / General
15.01.14

To *Desperation*

Acknowledgments

My friends Marti and Michele contributed greatly to the flow of this story, and I thank them both sincerely.

1

Friday Afternoon

Winifred Beatrice Kazlowski stood alone in her bedroom looking at herself in the full-length mirror. She was tallish at five feet, nine inches and slender without being skinny or poorly proportioned. A full head of dark hair, which shimmered with natural auburn highlights when the sun caught it right, framed a nearly perfect face. Straight nose, dark eyes, full lashes, strong cheeks, and perfect skin that showed only a few light wrinkles near her eyes until she smiled completed the picture. When she smiled, it only got better, even if the wrinkles deepened. As her gaze dropped and she inspected the rest of her body, she calmly accepted the fact that she had perfect breasts. Even under the black dress she wore, she could tell that they were firm, real, and what men would call perky: not too big and not too small. The fact that her nipples were pushing up through the fabric of the dress did not hurt the image either. Her flat stomach was tight, but she was not ripped like those girls in the exercise videos. She twisted half around and examined her rear. It was firm, round, and petite. She had worked on that over the years and unlike her stomach, it was, in fact, the product of a workout routine. A lot of her height was in her long legs, and these, too, showed no signs of wear and tear. Her skin was snug over the well-muscled, yet subdued and shapely, thighs.

Turning full to the front again, she smiled and thought, *You are one smokin' hot babe, even if you are hitting forty this week.* This was not arrogance or narcissism but just a simple statement of fact.

"Yeah. Too hot," she said aloud as she stood away from the mirror and pulled the dress back over her head. She tossed it on the bed and grabbed a bra. Once properly installed, she pulled on a tan blouse and reached for a pair of jeans. Pulling them on, she noticed that they were well fitting enough that her backside was still going to be a distraction. Tonight was her first date with Bob, and she didn't want to kill him. Off they came, and on went a set of dark slacks. Pulling her hair into a ponytail, she was able to destroy the *Charlie's Angels* look, but she shrugged; she was still pretty sexy. "Oh, well." She smiled. "There's only so much one can do." Not wearing makeup would not help diminish her looks. She never wore makeup. Maybe sometimes, a little eye shadow and subdued lipstick, but that was all.

Finally, she pulled out her digital tape recorder and slipped it inside her belt and into the pocket of her money belt. The recorder she had selected was flat and barely made the slightest bulge beneath the bottom of her waistband. She positioned it so that she could turn it on and off by putting her hand in her pocket. Of course, to do that, she had cut the bottom out of the pocket. That way, her slender fingers could feel the buttons on the recorder through the material of the money belt. She had been practicing around the house for months to make sure she got it right.

Everything had been fine until her husband, Noah, found it. He had not taken it well at all. But it was even worse when she finally told him that she was doing it for a class she was taking. She had explained to him quite a while ago that she wanted to start taking classes at the university just to improve her mind and stay sharp. It took a while, but eventually, he agreed that it might be beneficial. For her current class, she had told him that a big part of her grade was to conduct interviews with various people and then write a little story about what she thought about them. The course was in the marketing curriculum and was supposedly designed to help marketing agents understand their potential purchaser. The subjects, she said, were being selected by a job placement company in order to introduce variety and maintain anonymity for the student. The class would not work well if the subject knew they were being evaluated as a potential buyer. Unfortunately, most of the people already had day jobs, so the interviews needed to be done in the evening. In return for pretending to be an interviewee, the people being interviewed were going to get pointers on how to behave in an interview.

Noah still didn't like it. Taking one more glance in the mirror, she thought, just for a moment, that maybe her being hot was the only thing that had kept him from nixing her project. She rejected the idea. She liked to think that he loved her for a bit more than that.

The day he had found the tape recorder and she had told him about the class had been a pretty rough day, but she forced herself not to think about that now. She had to be ready for her date with Bob. Checking the mirror again, she admitted that she had been able to play down her looks a bit and now looked more like she wanted. It had taken almost ten minutes of work, but she had transformed herself from the formerly stunning beauty that she was, to one who was simply lovely to look at.

During her transformation, she reflected on the relationship she and her husband had. Noah had started a manufacturing plant using his inheritance. He opened it only a few months after he had graduated from college with his degree in mechanical engineering. They had already been dating all through senior year and the next step after opening the plant was to ask her to marry him. She had always admired the fact that he had known exactly what he wanted in life. She remembered that when they had first met, he had told her he was going to get his degree, start his own company, get a trophy quality wife, and start a family. She had taken the reference to "trophy quality" as a compliment since he had just asked her out on their first date.

In contrast to his technical degree, hers was in English literature, but she had actually found chemistry and chemical engineering to be interesting as well. She had even considered a minor in chemistry at one point. When she had become bored with her literature, she signed up for a Chem-E course to invigorate her mind. After they were married, she started working as the receptionist at her husband's business. The job saved money, which is important in a startup business. In that role, she found that her English degree was rather useful. In college, she had found that her interest in literature was in learning why people liked some books and not others. In her role as receptionist and partner, she used that knowledge to prepare an exceptionally successful set of marketing materials. Together, he knew mechanics and she knew marketing as well as what materials to use in the engineering designs.

She was good at being the receptionist and had spent almost fifteen years sitting behind that desk, greeting the customers and making them feel at home. Her pleasant attitude and good looks worked in favor of the business. When her husband finally brought them into his office, they were primed to be agreeable. Even though she ran the entire office, she often felt that Noah thought that her main role was to look hot and get the customers, most of whom were men, into the mood to be generous. Her role as sexy receptionist almost took a nasty turn on more than one occasion, but the worst thing about it was that she somehow always seemed inferior, even though it was her marketing that brought in the buyers.

These were special buyers. Noah ran a little production line stuff, but mostly, what he did was create new parts from raw blocks of copper, brass, steel, or iron. It was also part of her job to select the proper alloys of these metals. She had tried to get him into ceramics, but the process was too different, and he didn't want to retool. So he would bring in a client who needed a specialty part designed and then he would make one. Working with the client, he would build a prototype of the complete project, and when it was fine-tuned and considered finished, he got a fee plus 20 percent of the patent. Eventually, he did not need to invent any new items, but he still did so just because he liked it.

"Oh crap!" She had gotten distracted by her trip down memory lane and now really needed to focus. She was going to be late. But maybe that was a good thing, especially on a first date. *No*, she thought, and she took one last quick look at her notes, slammed the rest of her drink, and ran off to brush her teeth so she wouldn't smell like a lush when she met Bob.

Kissing her daughter Brea good-bye, she called back to Noah who was in his own study, "I'll be back in few hours, honey." She heard him call "bye" as she shut the door.

2

Bob

PJ's was a nice quiet place from Monday through Thursday. On Friday and Saturday, though, it turned into the hangout for the "I'm gonna be somebody someday" crowd of young professionals. Both the men and the women who were there were trying to find that middle ground between looking for business contacts and a hookup. Most of them had spent the last several years in college where they had been perfecting the art of seeking out potential mates. Whether that person was to be permanent or temporary didn't matter as much as the development of the arts of the introduction and of conversation. After graduation, they found themselves thrown into the business world, and they were applying the same skill set to a new goal: identifying a new business contact. As a result, at PJ's on Friday night, there was a lot of posturing and exaggeration going on. The challenge these new graduates had was to know when to suppress the hormones and when to let them run wild. PJ's was the perfect place. Low light, moderate music, good food, and reasonable prices on the drink menu created the proper mixture of atmospheres needed for either goal. Even though she was older than most of the other patrons, Winifred fit right in. Her self-assured carriage only served to heighten her attractiveness.

So this was Bob, she thought as she stood at the hostess stand at PJ's. Bob was easily identified by the gold tie and blue blazer they had agreed upon earlier. Bob was medium height and perhaps a tiny bit overweight, but not bad looking for a man in that stage of balding when the hair was what could only be described as wispy. He rose from the bar where he had been waiting and walked to the hostess stand just as Winifred told her she saw her companion. Bob had been guessing because there had been no agreed upon dress code for her. Not sharing that information was her way of maintaining a safe exit. She could always just claim not to be the woman he was looking for.

That little trick had been developed after her third blind date. She knew it would not be good the minute she walked into the restaurant. Jake, her date for the night, was rough. Really rough. Tattoos, a scraggly beard, and clothing that looked like he had mugged a homeless man to get them came together in a perfectly nauseating manner, but she had walked in wearing the tan skirt and saffron blouse that had been selected as the identifier and could not get away. After an evening of being talked at a little too closely, accentuated by a few wayward excursions by Jake's hand on her thigh, she had feigned being ill in order to get away. It was not a stretch. Ever since that night, she had made sure she knew what her men would be wearing while not telling them a thing about herself.

As Bob approached, she smiled and stuck out a hand, extending it well beyond hugging range. She had once had a bad experience with a hugger as well.

"Bob?" she asked. She could tell Bob was pretty happy with what he was looking at by the broad grin on his face. He nodded as she smiled and said, "Hi. I'm Winifred. People call me Freddie. I hope you weren't waiting long."

Bob only smiled and the hostess showed them to their table. When they were there, Bob pulled her chair out for her. *Well, at least he is a gentleman,* she thought. "So far, so good" went through her mind, perhaps more as a hope than an observation.

Bob seated himself and smiled some more. Under the table, her delicate fingers found the controls for the recorder, and she flipped it on. She knew what she was doing was illegal in Florida, but there were risks associated with this project. She knew them and accepted them. No one would ever hear these tapes except for her.

"So, Bob, were you waiting long?" she asked.

Bob shrugged his shoulders and just said, "No. Not really." He then fell silent.

Trying a new approach, Freddie asked, "Have you ordered a drink yet?"

Bob shook his head, slightly saying, "No. I waited."

Smiling, and giving Bob every chance to open up a conversation, she asked, "Have you eaten here before? Is the food good?"

Bob looked almost startled as he realized he needed to get the waiter or waitress over and get a menu. "No," he said. "I'll get a menu." Fortunately, the waiter was nearby and heard this subdued exchange. He popped right over with a menu and a list of the available adult beverages. Freddie knew already that she would need some help with this date, so she ordered a tequila shooter with lime and salt. It was a house special. Three tequilas in a little flight tray, which was really nothing more than a wooden slab with three places for shot glasses and a cup on either end for salt and lime wedges.

Bob started to look quizzical, and it was apparent he was rather lost when it came to selecting a drink. Instantly, Freddie knew she was going to have to take control of this date if it was ever to go anywhere, so she said, "Bob, let me get you something I know you will like." Turning to the waiter, she realized a date with him might be better than the one she had going with Bob, even though he was half her age. She read his name tag and said, "Tim, I would like my tequila flight to be a Patron Plata, a Tres Generacions Reposado, and an El Padrino Anejo. In that order. Bob, here, will have a Crown Royal, maple, with a glass of very cold water on the side. No ice. Make it a double." Freddie smiled at Bob. Bob knew he was not at liberty to ask for an alternative.

When Tim left, Freddie asked, "Bob, I take it you don't drink much. Is that right?" *God*, she thought. *I hope he's not a recovering alcoholic or something.* But Bob just shook his head and said, "No. Not much. What did you order?"

"I'll explain it to you when it comes." Freddie smiled. "Did you want to eat?"

Freddie watched Bob look at the menu and thought for a second that she was going to need to order his dinner too. But eventually, his face brightened a bit, and he pointed to the entry in the middle of the page, saying, "Got it." Then he beamed at her with an air of accomplishment.

Tim returned with the drinks and set them on the table, asking, "Have we decided on dinner? Or do we need a few more minutes?"

Freddie said, "I'll have the shrimp and pasta dinner in clam sauce." Bob just pointed again to the menu as Tim wrote something down and then left. The normal course of events was that there would now be a long wait between ordering and eating. The interlude was normally the best time for Freddie and her project. She had learned that drinking on an empty stomach would often lead her dates to engage in some really good conversation. It was a time when they could either open up to her or begin to make their moves. Whatever choice they made, it was always revealing. Tonight, however, she was a bit worried she would have to pry sentences loose from Bob one by one.

Freddie took Bob's Crown Royal and swirled it gently then pushed it toward him. "So, Bob, this is your drink. It is a fine Canadian whiskey with a bit of a sweet flavor to it. The water is either to add to the whiskey if you think it is too strong, or to drink afterward. That's what we call a chaser. Sometimes when I drink my tequila, I get an Everclear chaser." Studying Bob's face for any sort of reaction to her joke, and seeing none, she knew she was in trouble. "Here's the rule, Bob. You need to take a little sip, not a gulp, but a sip, and let me know how you like it." While Bob mulled that over, Freddie grabbed the Patron and slammed it, skipping both lime and salt. It was going to be a rough night.

When she put the shot glass down, she continued her explanation. "What I have here is a three-shot run of three different tequilas. Each one is a different brand and a different style. See the color? This one, the empty one, was clear. Remember? It doesn't have much flavor at all but is still recognizable as a tequila. The darker the color, the more flavor. Get it?" Bob nodded and took a sip of his Crown Royal. He winced. She had to remind him to take a sip of water.

"What do you do for a living, Bob?" Freddie asked. Bob just looked at her. Then he looked at her empty shot glass. Then back at Freddie. Looking at his own glass, he hesitated. "*No!*" Freddie said, just a little too loud for the restaurant's atmosphere. "Sip it, Bob."

Bob looked back at Freddie and said. "I deliver stuff."

"What stuff?" Freddie probed. Bob looked at his drink, took a tiny sip like he had been instructed to do, and said, "Body parts."

Finally, Freddie thought. We are getting somewhere. "Whatever do you mean, Bob?"

Bob said, "I am one of those guys that takes a liver from the morgue, throws it in a cooler, jumps in a Chevy Volt, and drives it over to the hospital where a patient who needs it is waiting. I hang around outside autopsy rooms way too much." Bob took a pretty long pull on his drink and choked. While getting his chaser of cold water he had to wipe tears from the corner of his eyes.

"Now that is interesting." Freddie offered with a grin and followed it with her second tequila. This one, however, was done with the style she had developed over the last few months. She started with a little lime. She applied it first to the rim of the shot glass, then directly to her lips, adding a final swipe of the lime on her tongue. This was followed by about half a shot and then a wet finger that had been stuck into the salt went into her mouth, where her lips closed around it with the full intent of being a sensual atomic bomb. She thought it might loosen him up a bit.

Bob just stared, slack-jawed, with maybe a little bit of drool, and said, "Yes, it can be. But mostly it's just a delivery service." Freddie knew she had gone too far and was wondering how to recover when Tim brought the dinner.

Bob finished his drink and his ice water while Tim placed the plates on the table. Freddie wondered how this would work out, since it was really clear now that Bob was not a drinker and may have already had too much. *No matter*, she thought. Her project was not about accommodating these guys so much as it was about documenting their natural state.

Dinner was sparsely sprinkled with conversation. Bob said he liked her hair and was embarrassed about his. He admired her healthy appearance and wished he had taken better care of his own body. He had never been married, and the longest he had ever dated anyone was for about six months, back in his twenties. By the time dinner and his second double shot of Crown Royal was finished, Freddie knew Bob inside and out. It was also clear that he had been drinking the whiskey in a pretty feeble and failed attempt to impress her. Freddie had stretched the last shot and a half of her tequila flight out over the ensuing dinner hour and was quite in charge of her senses, while Bob had taken his double in a display of poco macho, which took its toll on his composure.

By the end of dinner, Bob was a mess. He thought he was fine, like most people do when they drink sitting down, and didn't realize he was in trouble until he stood up. Bob did pay the bill, which was always a good sign, but then needed a bit of help navigating his way to the front door of the restaurant. Freddie was a little concerned, so she walked him to his car. It really was a Chevy Volt, and it really was dead. No gas. Bob had forgotten to fill up. No charge on the battery either because Bob had not plugged in. While Freddie waited with him for the cab, Bob got the idea that he was Bruce Willis or something and started getting way too close. Bob's hands started wandering and exploring even though Freddie was still trying to hold him upright, creating quite the dilemma. Should she let him wander or drop him in the parking lot? Bob was asking about a second date. Freddie didn't want to hurt him. He had obviously already been through the wringer with other girls, due in no small part to his own ineptitude as a charmer. She decided to deal with his hands one at a time and was quite relieved when the cab showed up. She put him in and gave the driver a fifty to get him out of there and home safely.

Going to her own car, she turned off the recorder, slipped an AC/DC disk in the player, and drove home. It wasn't late when she got there. Bob had sort of lost steam a little early in the evening, and she was earlier than expected. Noah met her at the door with flowers and a bottle of wine. "Hi, honey. I'm glad you're home early. Brea's already in bed asleep. How did the interview go?"

"It was fine, I guess. The guy isn't very interesting, but I will need to talk with him again," she said as she gave Noah a little kiss and relieved him of the flowers. "These are really nice," she added. She hadn't lied. They really were nice and she put them in some water. On the other hand, she thought, it was really too bad that after sixteen years, Noah still had not figured out she was not a wine drinker and preferred beer or tequila. She shared a glass of the wine with him and snuggled on the couch, making small talk until she fell asleep on his chest.

3

Saturday

Freddie woke up in her bed not really sure how she had gotten there from the couch. She hadn't been drunk, but she was really worn out from the long hours during the week and the stress of meeting Bob. It was immediately apparent that she had not brushed her teeth. Noah was not to be found, but he had left a note by the coffee machine. "Gone to play some golf. Angelique called and wants you to call her back. Something about Bob and some other people."

Freddie expelled a deep sigh of relief. Angelique was from the dating service that Freddie had told Noah was the job placement service. Angelique had been given instructions to call the private line in Freddie's office and to only refer to herself as being from "the service." She had been further instructed to say she had made an appointment, not a date. Freddie had convinced her that these code words were necessary because she was uncomfortable with Brea hearing one of the messages and learning that her mom was dating. Noah had heard the message as Angelique left it. He would never actually pick up her phone because he had no interest in who was calling. As he had once said to her with a great deal of irony, he "was not going to be her receptionist." In fact, that was the reason she had a private line in her study in the first place. Noah didn't like sifting through messages from the school and her friends.

Freddie dialed her number. "Good morning, Angelique. Freddie here. I got your message. Do you have another guy for me?"

"Hi, Freddie." Angelique virtually bubbled with unbridled enthusiasm for her work. "I have two more for you, but first tell me about Bob. Was he okay?"

"To be honest, I don't know yet. I want to see him again. To give him a fair shot, let's make it twice more, if you can set that up. I need to get to know him better." Freddie had not told Angelique about her project either.

"Well, dearie, you sure made an impression on him. He already called and said he wants to see you again. I will set something up for sometime next week. Would you like to know about Richard?" Angelique paused a bit then said, "He's your date for tonight if you think you can handle two in a row."

"Ha-ha...very funny," Freddie replied. "Of course I can handle two in a row. I could handle two like Bob in one night." She poured a coffee and said, "Tell me about this guy Richard."

"Unlike Bob, I think Richard has a bit of money in his background. He seems a little more cultured, almost proper, if you know what I mean, and he hints at having expensive tastes when I talk with him. He wants to take you to that rooftop restaurant down off the Tamiami Trail. You know the one with the view looking out over the Everglades?"

"Okay. That sounds like fun," Freddie said with a little too little enthusiasm. Sometimes this project just got tiring. She forced herself to perk up a bit and asked "What will he be wearing? What does he look like?"

Angelique paused a second as she looked for her notes. "Let's see. He is about six feet tall, 180 pounds, so skinny-ish, and will be wearing a blue blazer over a white shirt, with blue jeans. He wants to meet you at seven thirty. I'll tell you about the second guy later. I'm getting a call on the other line. He isn't available until next week anyway."

"Okay," Freddie said. "I'll let you know how it goes."

Freddie put down the phone, refreshed her coffee, and went into her study. Powering up the computer, she reflected on Bob. So quiet. So timid. And then all hands. She popped the cable connecting the digital recorder into the computer and downloaded the audio file. She labeled it "Bob_No_1.wav" and put it in folder labeled "dates." In another folder, labeled "Bob," she opened a text file and typed out some notes on the events of the night before. Still with her coffee in her hand, she then retired to the tub for a nice long soak with the latest Tom Clancy novel.

Just about the time when the bathwater was getting too cool to be soothing, Brea slowly opened the door. Like her mom, Brea was slender, but unlike her mom, she was not tall. Her hair was dark and short into something like a shaggy page boy. Sometimes, Freddie thought these years were the best. Brea was not quite eleven and had not yet entered the teen years she heard so many bad things about from her friends. Maybe Brea would be different, Freddie conjectured. Accepting reality, she realized her own teen years had been a bit wild, and she should expect the same. She decided to take the time to tell Brea about her own mistakes. That way, Brea might not have to make them too.

"Mom. Are you up?" "I've been watching the morning cartoons in my room because I didn't want to wake you."

Freddie waved her in. "Good morning, sweetie. Did you have a nice night last night with Dad? How was dinner?"

"Mom. Dad can't cook." Brea screwed up her face in a frown. "You know that. We had macaroni and cheese with a boiled hot dog. He said I can't have a bun because that would be another starch, and the macaroni was already a starch."

"Where does he get that stuff?" Brea crinkled her nose with the question.

"He reads a lot, sweetie," Freddie said as she extracted herself from her novel and her bath. "What else did you do?"

"What do you think?" Brea asked sarcastically. "We watched golf on television. I tried to get him to play Chutes and Ladders with me. He said he would after the match was over, but by then, it was bedtime."

Brea got her toothbrush out, and as she put the paste on it, she asked, "Are you going to be home tonight?"

Freddie wondered if her daughter missed her or if she was just concerned about dinner. "No, sweetie. I need to go out to a meeting again. I'm sorry. This project of mine won't last forever, though, and we can spend a lot more time together then."

"In the meantime, why don't we run over to the park and play some catch?" Brea smiled a big smile at this suggestion. She loved the park, and Dad hardly ever took her there. When he did, they did not play catch. He said it wasn't ladylike, whatever that meant.

Ten minutes later, Freddie was tossing a softball to Brea. "Come on, Mom!" Brea yelled. "Put some heat on it!" Freddie liked playing catch, but since Brea was just developing the coordination she needed, Freddie had been afraid to throw the ball overhand.

"Are you sure?" Freddie said. Brea nodded, and Freddie threw a slow looping ball in Brea's direction. Brea caught it with ease and tossed it back. With each throw, Freddie put a little more speed on the ball and the arc of the trajectory became flatter and flatter. Within a few minutes, Brea and Freddie were trading fastballs. They were both having a great time until Brea misjudged one, and it bounced off of the outside of her glove and into her forehead.

"Oh my God! Are you all right?" Freddie ran to Brea.

Brea had sat down hard when the ball hit her, but she was not crying when Freddie got there. She looked up at Freddie and said, "You always told me that progress included pain, Mom." She winced as she touched her forehead. "Now I know what you mean."

"Well, we're done for today," Freddie said.

"Uh-uh," Brea said, getting up. "I'm getting the ball and we are going to throw and catch ten times without a miss before we go in."

"Where did you learn that?" Freddie asked with a smile.

Brea jogged off to get the ball, pointing back at her mom, yelling. "*You!*"

Back in the house, Freddie started her normal routine of cleaning while Brea did her homework. When she finished, she threw together a shepherd's pie and stuck it in the oven. That way, Brea would not need to suffer through another hot dog and pasta meal.

Noah came back from the golf course only moments before Freddie needed to start getting ready to go. Apparently, he had spent a couple hours on the course and another couple, or more, hours in the nineteenth hole playing poker and bragging about his putts. She showed him where the dinner was and how to keep it warm in the oven until they were ready to eat and disappeared into her room.

Getting ready for the date with Richard was almost the opposite of getting ready for Bob. For Richard, she had wanted to look a little better, but still not crushingly beautiful. She could do crushing, but not on a first date. Not for this one anyway. Something in Angelique's description had put her on alert. She couldn't put her finger on it, but there was a hint of anxiety in Angelique's voice. Still, she needed to up her game for Richard because Angelique had described him as "proper." She needed something slinky. She wanted something tight-ish but not too tight. *It should be black*, she told herself. For accent, she selected gold earrings and a petite gold necklace. Heels would make her and Richard about the same height.

It was after six when Freddie emerged from the bedroom. Noah was eating dinner with Brea. When Freddie came out to the kitchen to say good-bye to Noah and good night to Brea, she saw Noah's face turn slightly red. "Honey, I know you need to go out for these interviews, but do you have to look so damn good doing it?"

"Please don't use foul language in front of Brea," she replied. "And, yes, I do. What I do relies on making sure the man is comfortable. It's just like at the office. Some people like casual, like Bob last night, and some…not so much. Tonight I am going to the Horizon Club down by the 'glades. I don't expect to be very late, but certainly past your bedtime," she said as she turned to Brea. She kissed Brea of the forehead and Noah on the lips and hurried out the door.

4

Richard

Her drive to the Horizon Club was uneventful. She had taken the Porsche Noah had bought her for her fortieth. It was still a few days early, but just in case Richard was from money, she didn't want to have him see her in the Ford. A Prius was all she had for years. Noah said it was a remarkable example of engineering, and she simply must have one as a corporate statement. Of course, he had his vintage Mustang: 1967. And that was okay for him because he had to have panache.

Cruising down Military Trail, which is the main thoroughfare south from their house, she prepared herself. *Focus*, she said to herself. The tape recorder was going to be difficult with this date. There really isn't much room in a slinky black dress for even the thinnest of electronic devices. Instead, she had slipped it into the pocket of her dinner purse. She would need to actually open the purse to operate the controls, but she had a plan involving lipstick.

Richard sat at the bar in the first floor lobby. The place was not what she had imagined. The bar was off to one side of a lobby that could only be described as cold. Marble floors, marble walls, an occasional armchair, and side table dotted the airy space, which was made even more so by the floor-to-ceiling glass of the front wall. Once again, she had managed to be five minutes or so later than the appointed time. She paused at the door and eyed him discretely. He was almost Latin looking. His dark hair was longer than most men wore it, especially after George Clooney set the new "short steel" hairstyle. Or was it Mark Harmon? She couldn't remember now. *God*, she thought. *What weird stuff goes through one's mind when commencing a job like this.* Subconsciously, she checked how her dress was riding, turned on the recorder because it seemed safer now than later, and strutted into the room. Oh, yeah. She knew how to strut. All she needed was to play that Bob Seeger song in her head, and it all just came naturally. "Oh, they love to watch her strut" went through her head, and the hips just started moving all on their own. By the time she reached Richard, in his Armani suit, long hair, and with his Basil Hayden bourbon in his hand, he was jelly. Or so she thought. She was wrong. The price of overconfidence was about to take its toll.

Still, the effect was not lost on Richard. He had noticed her just as she began the long, and sensuous, walk across the floor to the bar, and he could feel his pulse rate go up. Of course he had no idea that she was his date. The agency refused to tell him anything other than a name. They said it was to protect her. He knew it was just all part of the game and so went along with it. Still, she was walking right toward him and he hoped that this was Winifred from the agency and not some chick looking at the guy next to him at the bar.

Richard rose as she approached. She recognized the blazer and blue jeans look, and so she put out her hand and said, "Richard?"

Richard thought that any man in his right mind would be Richard for tonight if this lovely lady was to be his date, but he just smiled and said, "Yes. And you are Winifred?"

"Call me Freddie," she replied.

"Okay, Freddie, shall we go up to the roof?" Freddie was relieved when Richard guided her to the elevator, which would take them to the eighteenth floor where the restaurant was located. She was not interested in spending the evening at the lobby bar. The ride up was full of small talk and was in stark contrast to the awkward silences she had experienced with Bob. Richard was quite the conversationalist. At the top, when the elevator doors opened, the first thing they saw was the broad flat expanse of the Everglades. It was stunning, and almost in a daze, Freddie stepped out and toward the floor-to-ceiling windows ringing the restaurant. Richard was unfazed, for he had been here many times before. The elevator opened facing west and it was just before sunset. The sky was still bright blue but was accented with the rich pink and gold wisps of clouds common in south Florida. The Everglades stretched out for miles as far as the eye could see. Here and there were small treed islands, which made what looked like little green mounds in a sea of golden green grass. Way off to the south, an isolated thundershower made its way across the 'glades. She was looking at what would be the perfect postcard to send to her friends in Peoria.

Freddie was so taken in by the view that she had not realized that Richard's hand was at the small of her back. He was not holding her or caressing her, but he was just there. She thought it a bit early for that and made a mental note to watch him carefully.

A waiter appeared and began to say, "May I show you to your seat, Mr...." but Richard put a finger to his lips and said, "Careful, Tony. I told you about tonight. The agency doesn't like us to use last names."

Tony nodded and said "Yes, Mr. Richard" with a tiny grin. "This way please." Tony led them through widely spaced tables for two to one near a window. Freddie noticed the spacing of the tables and that there were only a few, which seated four people, and concluded that the place was designed for intimacy and discretion.

Unlike Bob, Richard let Tony hold her chair and then waited for Tony to hold his as well. Freddie noted it, thinking that Angelique had been correct. This guy had some money in his background.

Richard was a wine drinker. He preferred red over white, and Tony knew it. Tony apparently knew Richard pretty well. "I see you've been here before" was Freddie's opener. The ride in the elevator had proven that Richard was a conversationalist and she wanted him to talk. Freddie put her hand on her dinner bag and wanted desperately to assure herself that the recorder was on. She just needed an opening.

"I suppose I come here once or maybe twice a month." Richard lied, and Freddie knew it. Waiters don't get that friendly with a client at once a month. Richard probably came here once a week and probably always sat in Tony's section. He probably tipped pretty well, and that was partly why Tony seemed to fawn over him. This place was nice, but not at the level where all the waiters treated all the guests as kings and queens. *No*, she thought, *there is a relationship here.*

Tony reappeared with a bottle of Gamay. He and Richard went through the symbolic dance of smelling the cork and tasting it to make sure it was acceptable. No one ever sends wine back anymore. The art of storage had just outlived the danger of spoiling, but the ritual persisted. Freddie had no idea what a Gamay was, and completely breaking protocol, she asked to sniff the cork as well. Richard adjusted nicely, realizing that she was not familiar with it. "Gamay is in the Beaujolais family of wines. It is a bit sweet and not well suited for dinner, but then again, we have not gotten to dinner yet."

Tony poured them each a glass, and Richard indicated that he should leave the bottle. Apparently, Richard had no intention of getting to dinner anytime soon, and that suited Freddie just fine.

"So, Freddie, tell me a little about yourself" Richard opened with a classic but effective line. Freddie had to say something even if she wanted most of the evening to be spent with Richard talking and her listening.

"Well, let's see. I'm in my late thirties." This was still true for three more days so Freddie did not feel that urge to make a note about this for her next confession. "I'm a receptionist at a local engineering company, and I have a beautiful daughter who is going to be eleven years old this coming winter. I'm pretty much raising her on my own." *Dammit*, she thought. Was she going to have to go to confession for that? "She's at her dad's house tonight. I hope she's doing okay. She doesn't really like it when I go out." She had laid the foundation for a quick exit if she needed it and only told one small half of a lie. She never actually said she was a single mom, and she did raise Brea mostly on her own. Still, the implication was clear.

"Do you have children?" This was an odd conversation starter for most dates, but for people in their late thirties or early forties, it was pretty widely accepted that the relationship was not going to be the first for either of them.

"Oh no. I am childless," Richard said. "My work has kept me from being able to accept the responsibility of any children, and even if it didn't, I have not found the woman who would bear them."

Freddie kept her face in a firm but not noticeably rigid smile while thinking, *Seriously? What does this guy do that he is too intensely occupied to have children?* So she asked, "What is it that you do, Richard?" She liked to intersperse her date's name in the conversation every so often to tag the recording and make sure she would not be confused later. There were so many dates, so many men. It had become a bit of a challenge to keep them all straight.

"Well," Richard said, "I'm sort of a freelance consultant." By the look on Freddie's face, he knew this would not be enough, so he continued, "Okay, I can see that I need to go into a bit more detail. You're probably thinking what most people do when I tell them what I do, "consulting on what?" Well, the answer is that I consult on everything. Do you remember when newspapers used to have a thing called an information service?" He could see by the look on her face that she did not have any idea what he was talking about. "Newspapers used to have a guy with a computer who would take calls from the general public and try and find out the answer. I think it started as a means of helping the local teachers get their facts straight and then was thrown open to anyone. Anyway, people would call and ask things like 'How many territories does the US control?' or 'How many countries are in the UN?' People would call and ask how many ounces are in a gallon or what the difference was between a dry ounce and a wet ounce. That sort of thing. Well, when Al Gore invented the Internet, the service improved at first, but then, when Google came out, the market crashed. You can find remnants of it today in online services like Google Answers or Ask.com. I do that. I find answers for people."

"Are you a private detective?"

"Oh no. I just know how to look things up. But in truth, sometimes I do work for detectives as a consultant. You know, looking stuff up."

Freddie was worried but didn't show it. She had specifically told Angelique that she was not to have any dates with private detectives or cops. No law enforcement at all. Consulting was not technically the same as being a detective, but this guy did know how to look stuff up, as he said.

"Wow. That's fascinating. What's even more interesting is that you can actually make a living at it. I guess there are still a lot of people out there who can't navigate the Internet or go to the library."

Richard just sort of chuckled and said, "Good! Otherwise I would not have a job at all! Of course, things have been slowing down over the years, and actually they have been really slow lately. Last year, I only just made my six-figure goal, and this year will be a challenge too."

Freddie thought that it was interesting how he just happened to work into the conversation that he made at least a hundred thousand dollars a year.

"Really? That's too bad. I sure hope things pick up. Maybe it's a karma thing. You know, the ebb and flow of fortune? This year has been good to me. I'm still just a receptionist, but look over here." She brought Richard to the window and pointed down at her new Porsche. "I just got that for my birthday. Brand new and in definite need of being broken in properly."

She could tell by Richard's face that her gambit had paid off. His reaction to her both having a very nice and pricey ride while claiming to be in a low-paying job had spun him around. He was wondering if she was a hooker, a gold digger, or an heiress. Or maybe, he decided, she had just got a good deal in what he presumed had been a recent divorce.

Back at the table, the wine had been depleted, and the dinner had been served. Freddie was mad at herself because she had not been able to pick up her dinner bag and take it to the window, so she would need to make a mental note of the exchange and his reaction. The rest of dinner was filled with small talk, most of which was probably lies on his part and dodges on her part. It always went this way on the first date. For the men, lies, or at least half truths, were the fare for the evening. They could always be "clarified" on the second date if there was one. Freddie had already learned that the first date was mostly about getting a second date and that the second date was mostly about getting laid. That's how the male mind worked. Freddie had to constantly remind herself to let things play out and not prejudge people.

When Tony came to clear the table, Freddie took note of that too. It was almost unheard of that the waiter would host the entire evening. Tony had seated them, brought the wine, taken the order, served the meal, and cleared the table. Where was the bus boy? Richard rose and came around to help Freddie with her chair.

"Shall we go?" he asked. Freddie only wondered for a second about the bill and then realized Richard had an open tab. Yes, he came here more than once or twice a month. She entertained the notion that he might even be a part-owner but dismissed it quickly. If he had that much money, he surely would not need the services of the agency for his dates. In the elevator down, he reminded her that her new Porsche needed to be broken in and suggested that they take a ride out Alligator Alley. It was a very straight and flat stretch of road with very few law enforcement officers.

The bottle of wine before dinner and the second bottle during dinner had not dulled her senses so much that her internal alarms didn't go off when he suggested this. *No*, she thought. Driving out into the least populated area of the state in the middle of the night with a guy she just met was not in the cards. Fortunately, she "had an app" for that. Feigning a silent ring on her phone, she picked it out of her dinner bag and held it to her ear. "Uh-huh. Yes. I understand. I'll get there as soon as I can and take her home with me." As Freddie spoke, she once again felt that gentle pressure in the small of her back. Richard was about to make a move. Right there in the elevator. Putting the phone into her purse, she could feel the pressure getting a bit stronger, and she knew what was coming. She parried by looking straight into his eyes and putting a finger on his lips, saying, "Next time."

Her move would assure him that he would get a second date. She could get more information about him and he could get laid. Or so he thought when he nodded and said, "Okay. Next time."

Still one step ahead of him, Freddie said, "Just call the service" and stepped out of the elevator into the main hall of the hotel. Fully back in line, Richard walked her to her car without further transgressions.

When she got home, Noah was still up and apparently waiting for her. He greeted her pleasantly enough, but she could tell he was inspecting her for signs of dishevelment. Apparently, her choice of attire for the evening and the length of her date had started to bother him. She didn't really want him to feel that way. She really loved him. So she looked him in the eyes and said, "I saved all this for you, honey. There's no need to worry about me on these interviews. Now let's see if you are as good at undressing me as I am at getting dressed."

5

Sunday

Noah was still asleep when Freddie slid out of bed. Brea was in the kitchen making what she thought was breakfast, but Freddie knew there would be a mess to clean up too. Brea was independent and didn't want to wake up her mom unless she had to. She knew the kitchen rules quite well. She was allowed to make toast and cereal but not anything that involved the stove, like eggs, bacon, or oatmeal. Freddie had refused to get a microwave because she thought the food tasted odd, and now after years without one, she didn't miss it at all. Brea was also, on occasion, allowed to make coffee, and it was this aroma that had brought Freddie to life.

Years ago, when Brea was about five, Freddie had set down the kitchen rules. It happened one evening when Freddie was making spaghetti. Brea was curious about what was on top of the stove, but was still too short to see. Freddie saw Brea reach up toward a pot on the front burner and recalled with horror the stories she had seen about small children trying to see what was in a pot and spilling boiling water on themselves. Because Freddie felt that understanding was better protection than prohibition, she had picked up Brea and set her on the counter where she could see into the pot and also feel the heat. Freddie had explained the danger while satisfying Brea's curiosity. She even got a chance to stir the noodles. The rule was that Brea was not to reach up and over the stove until she could see into the pot without standing on tiptoe. She was not to reach back to the controls until she could do it without reaching over the pot. It was a good rule because Brea knew why it was a rule not because Mom "said so."

Today, Brea had followed the rules and had also exercised her independence in a very creative mixture of good behavior and pushing the limits. The pan was out and on the stove. Bacon was in the iron skillet, and four eggs were perched in the Styrofoam carrier beside a nonstick skillet with a couple tabs of butter already sliced and sitting in it waiting for heat. The biscuit mix was in the mixing bowl. Milk and blueberries were measured out and waiting in little cups. But the stove and the oven were still off.

Brea beamed a big "I got away with it" smile when Freddie came through the door. Both of them just started laughing out of control. Finally, there was a hug, some coffee for Freddie, juice for Brea, and then Mom turned on the stove to begin her part of what she was sure would become routine.

Freddie wanted to tease Brea a little about the kitchen activities. Instead, she decided that this would be a good place to act on her decision to share some of her mistakes with Brea. Not wanting to jump into it too suddenly, she laid the cornerstone. "You know," Freddie began, "and you know I know." She smiled at Brea. "You came very close to breaking some kitchen rules. It reminds me of when I was your age. I did some things that were sort of against the rules, but not quite." Tweaking Brea's nose, she added, "Maybe someday, I'll tell you what a bad girl your mom was." Freddie knew it would take a couple days, but eventually, Brea would ask her about her youth.

The area they called the kitchen was actually quite large. The stove was located in a marble-topped island fully equipped with two wooden cutting surfaces on either end. Beneath each cutting board was a compact refrigerator. One had chilled wine while the other had onions, peppers, and other vegetables that would need to be chopped before being added to a soup or a salad. That left lots of room in the side by side full-sized refrigerator-freezer for other perishables. Freddie was not fond of shopping and really enjoyed cooking spontaneously. To avoid crushing a cooking whim with a trip to the grocer, she had decided that her kitchen needed to be fully supplied at all times. The walk-in pantry completed her storage needs. On any given day, she could walk into her domain and impulsively decide what to make for dinner with fair certainty that she would have everything she needed.

As Freddie completed the meal, with Brea watching, and learning, intently, her mind went back to when Brea wouldn't even eat pancakes much less the shepherd's pie she had made last night. At first, Freddie's eclectic tastes had been a problem for Brea. Little children don't often like the same foods as adults. Freddie wanted to avoid Brea growing up as a picky eater and had been creative enough to find a way to deal with it. Freddie had explained to Brea that she didn't need to eat something as long as she tried it first. If she didn't like it, then that food item went on a list that was kept in the front of the cookbook. Brea liked this idea and had accepted it as a good deal. Once that part of the agreement had been reached, Freddie had explained that as children grew, their legs got longer, their arms got longer, and their taste buds grew. Older children grew more taste buds and different ones too. The new ones made food taste differently than it had before. They agreed that every year, they would tear up the list and started over.

About halfway through the pancakes, Noah joined them at the small kitchen table by the bay window that let light into the area. He seemed happy again and that was good. With her husband and daughter taken care of, Freddie excused herself and went to get her workout sweats. Ten minutes later, she was at full tilt on the treadmill in her office. The iPod was plugged in and playing a mix of the Who, Steppenwolf, and Led Zeppelin.

Halfway through The Pusher, she noticed that her phone was flashing. She decided that she was not going to be a slave to that stupid thing and kept on running. Twenty minutes later, she was listening to the message while doing her cool down walk.

"Hi, Freddie. It's me, Angelique. I have a date for you tonight and two more during the coming week. Tonight is a new guy. His name is Harold. Harold will meet you at the Twisted Cork for drinks at six. He's a high school teacher and will be wearing a lapel pin in the shape of an apple. He teaches history or economics or something like that. Then Monday, Bob wants to see you again. He will meet you at the Squid and Squint beach bar. Um…at seven. You should know that Bob was very apologetic and wants to make it up to you. Okay, that's two. Let's see. Oh yeah, here it is. The third guy is Terry. He's a couple of years older than you, but very nice. I interviewed him myself. I'm not sure what he does. He said he will meet you at PJ's. You know, that place where you went with Bob before. He is going to wear a Hawaiian shirt. Blue, with fish on it. Oh, yeah. Meet him at five thirty. Call me if you can't make any of these or if you have any questions. Have fun!"

Freddie pressed the off button and became aware that Noah had come into the room behind her. His look told her everything. "Not again tonight," he said. "Yes, honey, I'm afraid so. But like I told you before, I won't be doing this forever." He turned to go. Freddie called after him, "Didn't last night prove anything to you? Did it mean nothing?"

He softened and turned back to look at her. "Of course it did. It's just that this is hard with you being gone almost every other night. Brea and I miss you."

"I know," Freddie pleaded. "But you know this project is important to me, don't you?"

"I know," Noah conceded. "But that doesn't make it any easier. It seems like you're always busy now."

Freddie realized that she still worked forty to fifty hours at the office as the receptionist and manager. With this project of hers, she was out three or four nights a week, and when she wasn't out, she was locked in her study typing or reading. He complained again, "You said yourself that you barely have time to do the laundry and the shopping. It's taking its toll on us."

She nodded in assent. "True, honey, but we are strong, and we can get this done. And when we do, we will both be better than we are now. Now, since you mention it, I need to put the laundry in and go off to the grocer. I'll make sure and get some dinners that are already prepared so you don't have to make hot dogs again." She teased him about his cooking whenever she could but not to make him feel bad. She wanted him to try and learn to make simple dinners. "I'll take Brea with me so you don't need to worry about her."

Noah was still a bit dejected, but he said, "All right. We'll keep going, and I promise I will try."

As she wiped down the treadmill and dried the sweat from her face, she could hear him telling Brea to get ready to go to the store. Stripping off her sweats, she hit the shower. It was refreshing in there. It always was. It was also a bit of a torture chamber lately. In the shower, she was all by herself. The process of washing herself was a mindless routine, which gave her time to think about her life and her project. Sometimes she would even become meditative under the warm flow. She relished how her project could change her for the better. At the same time, she was beginning to wonder just exactly how strong Noah was going to be about it. If he could make it through, he'd be all right. They would be all right. She worried he would get too frustrated and set out some sort of ultimatum. He'd done things like that before, but not often. Noah was the kind of man who let you do whatever you wanted to do until it started to affect the things he needed you to do. He was that way with his employees, and he was that way with her. Under all this logical thought was a slowly rising and bewildering resentment of what Noah had said about needing time to do the laundry and go shopping. She wondered how long it would take him to stick some clothes in the washer if she just quit doing it altogether. She tried to rinse the thought away with the soap from her hair and not let it bother her.

Brea was a big help at the store. She was still only ten, but she was a smart and responsible young lady. Freddie took her time so that she would not speak of Noah in poor terms in front of Brea, but she methodically quizzed her on what prepared dinners Brea might be able to handle on her own. After a fair amount of chatting, the two girls mutually decided that stove-top meals would not be good right now. Both were a bit timid about hot liquids, which were not much below eye level for the petite youngster. The thought of reaching across a hot burner to get at something in the back was not a pleasant one for either of them. They did conclude, however, that oven items could be handled. The controls could be reached if it were not for the rule about reaching over a hot pot. Since the burners were not going to be used, Freddie decided that it would be okay to reach back there to operate the oven. Hot pads were already in place hanging on the cabinet door right next to the oven. Pot pies, fish sticks, baked French fries, pizza rolls, and even one or two actual dinners could be put in the oven. The most amusing part of the shopping trip was the argument about whether a frozen dinner could be pried out of its little plastic tray and put into a baking dish for the oven. The frozen dinner discussion made Freddie realize that she could make some casseroles or even lasagna, which could be heated up after she left. Most of the time, Freddie would be able to make dinner and then just leave it in the oven to stay warm. Unknown to Brea, Freddie was also using this time to get an update on where Brea thought her own kitchen skills were. Freddie was getting comfortable with what Brea felt comfortable doing in the kitchen. It was sort of a female bonding moment.

Back at home, once the groceries were put away, Freddie turned her attention to her date. Noah had left for the day. There was a note saying he was going to catch a matinee. She hoped he would be back before she had to leave. Maybe he was planning on being late to torpedo her? No. She shouldn't think like that. Turning her thoughts back to Harold, she wondered what a teacher would want in woman. He would want her to be smart. He would want her to be interested in kids. But what should she wear? How should she dress? One clue was with the lapel pin. He was going to be wearing a jacket. He would be subdued. *Hmmm…teachers*, she thought. *Would he want subdued or would he be sick of subdued?*

Okay, she thought. Let's go by the numbers. He is around seventeen- and eighteen-year-old girls every day. Can she compete with them physically? Realizing that there was a sick implication in that thought, she tried to bury it. The truth, though, was that every day, these girls decided what to wear, the intent was to attract the attention of the boy in the next row. Teachers were not supposed to notice, but she was sure that they did. The difference was that these girls were still acting like children, not adults, no matter how they dressed. Still, she asked herself if she wanted to make an impression with her body or with her mind. "So what if I go professional?" she asked herself. "What about a pants suit?" It was decided: charcoal gray, with a yellow scarf for a splash of color.

Noah did not get home on time. Freddie was not to be derailed, however, and she called Brea's best friend's mom. "Hi,

Pauline, this is Freddie. I was wondering if you could do me a favor. Noah's gone out and is not back yet, and I need to go to a business meeting. Can Brea come over and play with Sarah for a couple hours?"

"Great. Thanks," Freddie said into the phone. "I'll bring her right over. As she hung up, she saw Brea and knew she had overheard. "Sorry, sweetie. I need to go out, and Dad's not home yet. You don't mind, do you?"

Brea said she would love to visit Sarah, but inside, she was feeling a mixture of happiness, because she was going to her friend's house, and dismay, because once again, Mom had to work. Freddie knew it and realized that leaving her alone this much was a heavier burden on Brea than it was on Noah. "It won't be long, sweetie, and I will be done with this project. Just hang in there," Freddie said, giving her a hug.

Freddie dropped off Brea at Sarah's and sent a text to Noah, letting him know where she was. She was thorough, though, and virtually demanded that Noah reply before she left.

6

Harold

The Twisted Cork was one of those restaurants that catered to families more than singles. It had been converted from one of the chain restaurants. While the name had changed, the cookie-cutter layout of a central bar with booths and tables surrounding it had been left in place. Freddie arrived about five minutes early and took a seat on one of the benches outside. It was a pleasant night in Dania, Florida. The weather was not too cool, and as a result of a rare weather pattern, the humidity was low too. Sitting outside was not a problem. She struck up a conversation with another couple and waited—primarily so that she wouldn't look like she was alone. She had selected a seat far enough from the door that Harold would not walk directly past her but close enough so that she could keep an eye on people as they arrived. She had decided that she wanted to see this teacher before she met him.

And there he was. Right on time, as if there was a bell about to ring.

Freddie excused herself from her conversation and managed to get directly behind Harold as he entered the bar. Harold was tallish with a full head of dark hair. There was just a little gray around the temples. *Not bad looking*, she thought. Harold got to the hostess podium and was about to ask if anyone was waiting, when Freddie tapped him on the shoulder from behind. He turned slowly. Actually, he turned in a rather stately manner, with a bit of a scowl on his face, and Freddie immediately knew what it would be like to be in his classroom. She pitied the teen who distracted him from his lecture and received that stare.

"Harold?" she asked and smiled.

Once he realized that this lovely woman was to be his date, he softened and almost smiled. "Yes. And you are Winifred, I presume?"

Freddie flashed her best teenage smile and said, "No one calls me that. I'm Freddie."

"Your name is Winifred, young lady. Are you ashamed of it? Fred is a man's name after all, and you are certainly not a man. Even though you are wearing pants."

Freddie was a bit taken aback by this and failed to provide an answer in the allotted time. As they were shown to their table, Harold continued, "There are some rather famous Winifreds, you know. Winifred Atwell was a boogi-woogie pianist. Winifred Ann Taylor was the Baroness Taylor of Bolton, and Winifred Bamford-Hesketh was the Countess of Dundonald. Winifred Brunton and Winifred Nicholson were both famous painters. There is Winifred Holtby, Winifred Lewellin James, and Winifred Mary Letts who are all rather accomplished writers. Winifred Herbert was a famous British criminal. In fact, the first American woman to ever receive a PhD in mathematics was a Winifred. That would be Winifred Merrill. Perhaps the best known, though, is Winifred Baker who is, hmm…or was…the president of the Mozilla Corporation. You know. The one that makes the Internet browser Firefox?"

Harold paused briefly and then added, "So why are you ashamed of your name again?"

Freddie sat and looked at the waiter, "I think I am going to need a little something to drink, please. El Padrino. Anejo. Neat."

Harold told the waiter he would like a glass of the house Port, and the waiter went off to fetch Freddie's salvation and Harold's wine. "You know, Harold has a bit of a history too. It stems from the old English name meaning something on the order of a military leader. If it is spelled wrong, you know, with an 'e' instead of an 'a,' it means nothing more elegant than a messenger. I suppose sometimes it could be a harbinger, but since we have such a good word already for, um, harbinging…" Harold laughed at his own joke and continued, "Why would we confound things?"

Freddie knew the question was quite rhetorical and just smiled as he went on. "The name Harold actually fell into disfavor after King Harold endured that messy loss at Hastings to the Normans. After that, it was a fairly uncommon name until about 150 years ago. I sort of like it. I can relate to it. In my classroom, I am the leader, and my classroom is my kingdom."

Absently, Harold straightened the dinnerware, aligning the decoration on the butter plate so that the little crest was at the top and arranging the silverware in perfect order with perfect and equal spacing between each one. "You really should look into this and see if you can learn to like your name. You know, if I am not mistaken, there is actually a Saint Winifred as well."

Freddie's tequila came, and she put it straight down while Harold more or less toyed with his Port. Sniffing and savoring the aroma. She looked back at the waiter and, putting on her best English accent, said, "Please, sir, I want some more." The waiter smiled and nodded. He had apparently heard the Oliver Twist quote before. Harold snorted with a stifled sort of laughter that sounded like a pig with its nose in a trough. At least she had been able to make him laugh.

"You know," Harold said, "that I am doing this all wrong? Well, at least according to the book, it is wrong." He looked up from the swirling Port and saw that she had no idea what he was talking about. "You see, a Port wine is supposed to be an after-dinner wine. A dessert wine if you will. It is sweet and heavy, like a dessert, and is meant to be a sort of capstone to a culinary masterpiece. But you see, I am a renegade, a maverick, and like my name implies, I do not follow. I lead. I find my own way and tradition be damned."

Freddie struggled for something to say. Her pause was apparently too long because Harold continued. "Did you know this is from Portugal, not France? Most people think all wine comes from France and that Italians only stole the recipe, but Port, or Vinhos do Porto, is unique to the northern regions of Portugal. In fact, in Europe, it is illegal to label a wine as a Port unless it was actually made in Portugal."

Freddie decided to try and get into the conversation. "Oh, you mean like when they label something as a Napa Valley wine?"

Still looking at his wine and not at her, he began his retort. As he did so, Freddie made a mental note that he seldom looked at her during conversation. It was as if he was all alone in the world and was just talking. Perhaps he talked more to himself than to others. She wondered if this was how he conducted his classes. Maybe, she thought, it was easier on him to avoid looking at the students than it was to see what they were doing and feel obliged to ask them to behave.

"No, no. Not at all. But I can see where you became confused. What you should have asked is if this was like Burgundy wine or a Beaujolais. That would have been a much better question. You see, Napa Valley is just a place where Americans grow grapes and try to make wine using ancient European techniques. Burgundy wine can only be grown in Bourgogne, which of course is a region in France. Beaujolais is the same except that the Beaujolais region was not always in France. In the Middle Ages, when these were all loosely aligned fiefdoms, Beaujolais was sometimes in the French aggregate and sometimes in the German aggregate." Without seeming to take a breath, he went on. "Now here's an interesting fact."

Freddie thought to herself that she should have a notebook and a pencil but then grinned impishly as she remembered she was recording all of this. Harold did not notice her smile because he was still in the "looking glass" that the ripples of his Port had created. Perhaps, Freddie thought, she had actually found the White Rabbit.

"In Europe, as I mentioned, only a wine made in Portugal can be labeled Port and only a wine made in the Champaign region of France can be labeled as Champaign. In America, if a grower wants to make a wine using the right grapes and the Portuguese technique, he can label it as a Port. But when those Napa Valley people you mentioned make a bubbly wine using the technique for Champaign, they can't label it as a Champaign. It is labeled as a sparkling wine. One rather well-known company has resisted these label laws. Korbel makes a very good sparkling wine and labels it California Champaign. Another is Russian River Champaign. By putting the adjective in front of the Champaign, they have found a loophole in the law."

Harold paused for a sip of his wine. But the recitation did not stop. "Did you know that the Korbel winery was founded by three Czech immigrants? In the mid-1800s, three brothers found their way out of Czechoslovakia and into California. Their tale of hard work and ultimate success should be required reading in every economics class in America. Of course, I do touch on it in my social studies class, but it would be nice if the lesson were reinforced."

Finally, Freddie thought, an opening. "Is that what you teach, Social Studies?" She looked at him for some sort of assent and received a small nod, tilted slightly sideways. "I have a question about that? When I was in school, we were taught history and civics. My friend who has a teenage daughter says that they don't teach history in high school anymore, just Social Studies. Is that true?"

Still not looking at her, Harold launched into his explanation. "I think what you are trying to ask is whether or not our youngsters are getting a good education in history. Some schools still have classes titled as History, but most have titled them as Social Studies, so your friend is correct there. Another question you might have asked is why Social Studies, History, and Civics were different in the first place and why they have been combined now."

Freddie was able to interject a quick, "Yes, that's a better question" followed with an under her breath "I suppose" as Harold continued. "You see, when I first started out as a teacher, History, Civics, and Social Studies were all different classes. History was the study, or more accurately the memorization, of what happened. Social Studies was the study of societies, which provided the answers to why historical events took place. Civics was the class where teachers taught kids how to participate in the local community. Civics classes were supposed to teach kids how to be good citizens. Eventually, educators learned that teaching why history happened at the same time as actually what events took place gave the students a more complete understanding of our world. History and Social Studies merged. James Michener actually did a lot to tie those two things together with his novels. He actually made history interesting the same way that Thor Heyerdahl made archaeology interesting. Of course you know who Thor Heyerdahl was, don't you? He was the real live Indiana Jones!"

"What happened to Civics?" Freddie was finally able to interject.

"Civics has gone by the wayside. In fact, in a recent *Huffington Post* article I read, only nine states still had a Civics requirement for high school graduation. I'm not one hundred percent sure about why this was dropped, but I think that teaching the art of citizenship just became too political for administrators to deal with and so they skip it. I know that the principal at my school would have apoplexy if anyone mentioned anything political in a classroom, even if it was only to mention that we have several parties and that most seniors can probably vote in the election after they graduate."

Dinner came and went as Harold went on. Freddie had asked how Harold could teach the Social Studies-History hybrid classes without getting into the politics of either current or historical events. She asked how he could teach about the American-led coalition of forces invading Iraq and deposing Hussein without getting into the politics. Everyone in Freddie's age group knows that the US military invaded Grenada, but no one really knows why. Would her children know that the US invaded Iraq and not know why? Was this the future of American education? Harold's answer was lengthy, complete, and conducted without more than a random glance in her direction. His lack of eye contact during conversation was actually a bit unnerving. It left little to wonder about why he needed a service to get a date. As plates were being cleared, he was off on a lecture about the United Nations. Freddie had brought up the parallel between the formation of the United States for a better America with the formation of the United

Nations for a better planet. Harold's reaction to this concept was a mixture of horror that she could be so naïve and anger that such a concept was so widespread.

"Look. There is a huge difference between the US and the UN, and the difference is what makes America work and the UN a failure. A friend of mine once wrote, and I quote, that, *These United States have joined together of one purpose and of one set of principles and of one form of government among the members and of one goal, that of Life, Liberty, and the Pursuit of Happiness.* The key word in that sentence being 'one.' America works because the people and the nations, which most people erroneously refer to as colonies, had great similarities in their beliefs about government. They converted these similarities into one form of government. In the UN, there are dictatorships, juntas, communists, socialists, monarchies, and a rather wide variety of what are rather loosely referred to as republics. The nations share very little, and therefore, the UN will eventually do one of two things. It will become a one-world oligarchy, or it will fall apart."

"Now, before I forget, we need to go back to Thor Heyerdahl…"

Harold talked about Heyerdahl for a while, then Amelia Earhart, Charles Lindbergh, Roald Amundsen, and even Marco Polo as he related what seemed like an encyclopedic summary of explorers and adventurers who undertook their escapades in the name of science. At the end of the evening, Harold was kind enough to walk Freddie to her car, although he never actually stopped talking until she had closed the door and started the engine.

Noah and Brea were both fast asleep when Freddie got home. As quietly as she could, she got herself ready for bed and slipped in beside her husband without waking him.

7

Monday

In the morning, Noah was out of bed before Freddie woke up. When she saw the time on the clock and got up to go make coffee, she found him in the kitchen with Brea. He had only just started to make breakfast and had pulled out some bacon, eggs, and muffins. Freddie gave him a kiss on the cheek and said she would take over. This was not condescending on her part at all. It was what Noah wanted. He was not domestic.

Brea finished her breakfast and hurried off to get ready for school. As Freddie cleared the table, she mentioned to Noah that he she had another interview to conduct. Noah didn't say anything, but he did give her a nod before he left for work.

Needless to say, the office environment had become more and more strained since Freddie started her project. She diligently sat at the receptionist desk and made visitors and clients alike feel comfortable. In many ways, since her project started, this part of her job description had become counterproductive. In the past, Noah relished the fact that his clients spent a little too much time at the receptionist desk. But her evening interviews seemed different, and he did not enjoy it. Maybe it was because he was not in the next room. The thought had crossed his mind that he ought to follow her, but he knew he would get caught. That too seemed counterproductive. Noah also knew that what was bothering him was more than just the fact that his rather attractive wife was going out on these interviews, and going alone. He just couldn't put his finger on it.

Noah had done what he thought was his best to be a good father and husband. He had built a successful company, which provided a rather respectable income. He had purchased a very nice home for his wife and daughter to live in. He was paying an absurd amount of money to send Brea to a private school. Sure, he acknowledged to himself, he had convinced Freddie to drive a Prius for public relations purposes, but that was part of the business. So was having Freddie as a receptionist. Sometimes he wasn't sure if she really understood that part, but the fact was that the small talk that was elicited by her friendly smile and flawless looks had been a source of information that he used in his dealings with his clients. These conversations she was having during these interviews were of no use to him at all.

8

Bob

Noah had stayed a bit late at the office while Freddie had collected Brea from school. Freddie decided to make baked chicken and potatoes with green beans in a casserole dish for Noah and Brea. Brea sat at the kitchen table doing her homework while Freddie made the dinner. Brea and Freddie had a routine worked out where Brea would do her homework in the kitchen so that Freddie was right there for help if it was needed. At the same time, when an important part of the preparation was going on, there would be a time out on the homework, and Freddie would explain what she was doing. As she finished preparing the meal, she put it in the oven to stay warm. Brea was not quite finished with her reading assignment and so would need to stay at the table a while longer. Freddie told her that the dinner was going to be warm when she finished her reading. She needed to remember to turn off the oven and use the hot pads when it came time to eat. Brea was to wait for Daddy to get home so he could supervise her doing this. Then Freddie went to get ready for her date.

In the bedroom, Freddie struggled with what to wear. This was Bob's second date and he had gotten a little out of control last time. She made a mental note to make sure to watch his drinks. Angelique had said he was contrite, so maybe he would be better this evening. The Squid and Squint was a mid-range beach restaurant with a little bar and a live band that played out on the deck. She chose shorts, sandals, and a lightweight blouse.

The evening with Bob did not go well at all. Bob had chosen this particular bar in an attempt to look a bit more contemporary than he really was. The Squid and Squint was clearly not the type of place that a man like Bob would normally frequent. It was a place where beach bums, surfers, and tourists went for live music, seafood, and a hookup. Fortunately, it was a place where the music was more reggae than rock, and the recorder tucked in her shorts was still able to pick up the conversation. What there was of it was the same as on the first date. Freddie had to drag details from Bob, and Bob only offered one-word replies, never initiating a new topic. Freddie had briefly wondered why she had even agreed to a second date but then realized that getting to know Bob was very important to the success of her project. So she put up with it and did her best to draw him out. Bob, on the other hand, had little interest in getting to know Freddie. Bob's interest became clear as the night wore on. He had not had much to drink because Freddie had made sure to manage the evening's libations to avoid a repeat of last time. But still, as she and Bob exited the bar, Bob took her hand and said, "So where would you like to go? Do you want to go to my place? A motel? There's a nice one just up the beach there."

Freddie was a bit taken aback because this was the first initiative he had taken all night. "Bob, I hope you don't think I am going to sleep with you. This is only our second date." Bob looked crushed, surprised, and confused all at the same time. "But I thought the agency was sending me a, you know, a date."

Freddie said, "Yes, that's right. A date. Nothing more. Why would you think…? Did you think that I was a—what—a call girl?"

"Well, Angelique said that if I behaved myself, I might do better than last time." Bob offered in his defense. "For what the agency charges for these dates, I certainly thought there would be more to it than dinner and drinks, which I also had to pay for."

Freddie was now torn between being angry with Angelique for giving Bob a false impression and extreme pity. Bob was, after all, a basically nice guy. He just had no social skills, very little charisma, and little self-esteem. The three tended to form a vicious cycle, each one feeding off of the other. She wondered about Bob's background and how he got to be the Bob she knew. She wondered if he was like this in high school or if this personality was the result of other life events.

"Well, Bob, I am sorry if you had the idea that you were going to get laid tonight, but that doesn't mean I don't find you an interesting person. So let's leave it at this. You go to your place and I will go to my place and we'll give it two weeks rest. Then we can go out again and see what happens. Okay?"

Bob was crushed, but he agreed and walked Freddie to her car. As she got in, she told Bob, "Please don't say anything about this to Angelique. Just let me straighten it out with her."

Bob nodded, and Freddie knew he would do as he was told. He was just that kind of guy. On the drive home, she wondered about the wisdom of another date with him, but her project required a minimum of three dates unless there were extreme circumstances. In Bob's case, the extreme circumstance was a false impression, which only served to make Freddie want to give him another chance at being himself.

9

Freddie's Birthday

Tuesday morning, the smell of bacon and pancakes, interlaced with hot coffee, brought Freddie from her sleep. She opened her eyes and saw Brea with a breakfast tray. Noah stood beside her with his hand on her shoulder, while he held the coffeepot. "Happy birthday to you..." They sang in complete disregard for the tune or any semblance of harmony.

"Look what we made you for your birthday!" Brea said. The top pancake in the stack had a little smiley face in it made from blueberry jelly. The bacon was sandwiched in between the pancakes in crisscross layers, and to the side was a single cupcake with "40" on it. Brea saw Freddie's crinkled up nose and said, "It's your birthday. According to the rules, you have to try it, but if you don't like it, I won't make it again until next year." Freddie and Brea got a good laugh out of this while Noah just sort of looked puzzled. He never understood Freddie's parenting style and spent little time trying to do anything more than stay out of her way.

Apparently, Brea had planned most of the day because when breakfast was over, she announced that they were now off to play putt-putt golf. Noah liked real golf, but he put up with one day of putt-putt as a gift to Freddie. It was a good gift, but it might have been better if he had omitted the running commentary about it not being golf. At one point, Freddie took him aside and told him in hushed tones so Brea would not hear. "No, Noah, it isn't golf. It's people enjoying each other's company. The dinosaurs and windmills are nothing more than an excuse to hang out together."

This concept had not occurred to Noah. He said. "Oh. I guess I can see that. Am I over par in the 'enjoyable company' department?"

Freddie forgave him in part because of his joke. He really did try, but sometimes she had to show him the way. "You need to birdie the back nine if you want to ride home with us," she chided him back. He smiled and did his best to adjust his attitude.

Golf was followed by an ice cream, as was the custom, and Brea managed to embarrass Freddie by inducing everyone in the ice cream shop to sing "Happy Birthday" for her mom. Noah didn't mind this as much because once it was announced, Freddie's cone was free as a gift from the shop.

Noah had suggested that the two of them go out for dinner, but Freddie quite truthfully convinced him that she had been out so many times recently that a nice home-cooked meal would be a better present. He agreed as long as she prepared it, because, as she knew, the kitchen was not his home turf. Freddie accepted the deal and turned her task into more kitchen fun with Brea. The two of them spent an hour in the kitchen cutting and chopping and mixing all sorts of somewhat unlikely ingredients into a big pot that Freddie assured Brea would contain jambalaya after two hours of simmering. While they waited, they decided to adjourn to the couch for a matinee on the big screen. When the two girls got to the lounge, they were both surprised to see that Noah had placed a rather large bouquet of flowers on the table in acknowledgement of her birthday. The pancakes, golf, ice cream, movie, and jambalaya had made the day very nice for Freddie. It wasn't until after Brea had gone off to bed that Noah asked about the rest of the week's schedule. Of course he was upset when Freddie told him that she had class the next evening.

Freddie did not really like going out on a weeknight. She didn't like having to leave Brea at home and didn't really like having to explain to Noah all the time about the need to be away, so sometimes she told him she was in class at the university. She struggled with whether telling him this was a lie or not because she really was taking classes at the university. It's just that Wednesday night was not a class night. It was about two years ago that Freddie had decided to get her master's degree. She didn't really have a plan to do anything with it when she started. She just thought it would be fun to go back to school. As her studies progressed, however, she realized the value in it and became committed to the degree. Her formal classes had ended a while back, but she had not told Noah. Instead she had told Angelique that Mondays and Wednesdays, which used to be class nights, were good date nights. She still had her independent studies to finish, and she worked on these during slow times at the office and at home in her study after Brea went to bed. Noah hadn't really liked the idea of her going back to school, but he couldn't come up with a reason not to do it. Freddie expected that the company would benefit as well. She had already proven to be a reliable resource in marketing, and her advanced education could only improve her skills.

Still, Noah didn't like the idea. He couldn't really say why. He just didn't like it. Once, he had even taken the time to think about why he didn't like it, but he couldn't come up with a reason that made sense to him. He finally just let it drop, accepting his position as it was—without reason.

10

Terry

Freddie walked into PJ's at five thirty-five looking for a guy in a blue Hawaiian shirt with fish on it. Knowing what her date was wearing had turned out to be a blessing. The original intent had been so she could identify him before he could identify her. The blessing was that she could select something close to what he had and reduce any tension caused by mismatched wardrobes. So for Mr. Hawaiian shirt, she had chosen what could only be described as a sun dress. She figured the Hawaiian would be pastel, so she selected a pastel as well, but chose a peach to offset his blue. She picked him out of the crowd at the bar. He seemed harmless enough, so she tapped him on the shoulder and said "Hi. Terry? I'm Freddie."

When Freddie got a good look at his face, which had been somewhat obscured by the bar lighting, she almost turned off the recorder thinking the night was going to be a disaster. She remembered Angelique telling her that Terry was a few years older than she was, but it was apparent that he was at least sixty-five. He was in fair shape and not a bad-looking man, but he was way outside the parameters she had set with the service. Terry was literally old enough to be her father. In hindsight, the evening with Terry was actually quite enjoyable, although Freddie swore she was going to kill Angelique when she saw her. She was also glad that she had left the recorder on because Terry actually contributed to the project.

Terry was a retired steel worker from Pittsburgh. That's why Angelique wasn't sure what he did. He didn't do anything. His wife had died a couple years back, and he was just lonely. Other than his age, though, he was just like the rest of her dates. He wanted to get laid. Fortunately, Freddie was able to dispel his hopes early in the evening, and after that was settled, they actually had a nice time. He told her about what it was like to work high steel in a steel town. When he was younger, the work was actually harder because the smog had made it hard to breath. A couple hundred feet up in the air, there was often a layer of black soot with flecks of yellow in it that seemed to just hang there. He told her it was the worst in the summer, when there was no wind. It had taken its toll on his health, he told her. He had a lung disease of some sort and didn't really expect to be around for too many more years. So he just savored the time he had by fishing and going to the beach. He said he had called the service just to get some companionship. At the end of the evening, Freddie even gave him a little kiss on the cheek before leaving.

11

A Bad Day at the Office (Thursday)

The next day, Freddie found time to take a coffee break around ten fifteen. The agency opened at ten, and she was eager to speak with Angelique. She poked her head into Noah's office and told him she was going to get some air and a cup of coffee. She offered to bring him some, but he said he had just finished one. As soon as she hit the parking lot and was out of earshot of anyone, she dialed Angelique.

"The guy was at least sixty-five!" She almost yelled. She tried to control herself because she wasn't entirely sure no one was around. "What the heck are you doing?" she continued. "I told you I wanted men between thirty and fifty. No exceptions."

Angelique calmly said, "Freddie, what am I supposed to do with him? He was in pretty good shape for his age, and I don't have any girls in their sixties. If I didn't find someone for him to go out with, I was going to be fired."

Freddie didn't exactly believe her, but softened a little bit. "Okay, I know you have a job to do. He did pay for dinner, so all it really cost me was time, but no more, okay?"

"All right. No more. I do want to ask you about him, though. Some of the other girls said he was really good in bed. I swear I didn't know about that when I set you up with him. I got calls yesterday from two of his previous dates who wanted him back again. Can you corroborate that so I can tell his next date what to expect?"

Freddie's mind went into overdrive. "What do you mean? He told me he had a lung disease and had trouble breathing. How could he be that good?"

"Uh-oh," Angelique said. "That's not right. His last date said they played tennis before hitting the showers, together of course." She paused.

Freddie spat her words out. "That son of a bitch was going for a pity piece!"

Freddie didn't know what to say but decided right then that she would not erase the recording of their evening. As soon as she hung up, she realized that she had forgotten to ask Angelique what the hell she had told Bob that made him think she was easy. Well, she could let that go for now. She did, however, get out her notebook and wrote a quick summary of her conversation and about Bob's expectations. As she finished, she got a text from Angelique. It seemed that Richard had sent a bouquet of flowers to the agency to be delivered to her home address. Jenny, the other girl at the agency, knew the policy about not giving out a home address, but thought it would be all right to let the florist have it.

Freddie assessed the situation and realized that she was going to be in deep trouble if she didn't intercept the flowers. The vision, or nightmare, of Noah coming home to find a bouquet on the front porch with a note to her from Richard was more than she could bear. She couldn't leave the office without some sort of an excuse. By the time she got back in the building, she had a plan. Back at her desk with her coffee, she pulled up a spreadsheet with last month's expenses. She studied it for a minute and then found exactly what she was looking for. "Noah," she called. "Can you come here and look at something real quick?"

Noah emitted a muffled "yes," and soon arrived to stand behind Freddie as she pointed to the screen. "See this charge at Bailey's? Was that a client lunch? I need to know because the IRS will only let me take half of it as a business expense, and none of it if it was only you."

"Yeah, that was Jerry from Southern Avionics," Noah said. "He had some sketches of a new stepping motor controller and thought it would be easy enough to go over it on their table as on our conference room table."

Freddie removed her finger from the screen, and as she lowered her arm, she deftly dumped her coffee on her thigh. She had already drank most of it, and it had cooled so as not to give her a burn, but it did make a big dark spot on her pants. "Oh, crap!" She jumped up and used a prepositioned napkin to wipe her slacks and the floor as well as she could. "I need to go home and change. Can you survive without me for a while?"

Noah said, "Well, it's almost eleven. Do you want to just take an early lunch, and I'll go with you? Jimmy in drafting can answer the phone while we're gone."

Freddie's mind screamed, but her voice said quite calmly that she had received a call earlier that Spencer Ford, one of their design clients, was going to stop by around eleven thirty to go over some design specifications. She said she was sure she had put it on his calendar, but after a strategic pause, she admitted that maybe she had forgotten. Freddie offered to bring Noah some take out for lunch and said she would be back as soon as she could. On the drive home, she waited till exactly eleven twenty-five then called Noah to tell him Spencer had called to say he couldn't make it after all.

At home, she saw the florist just leaving. It was not a florist. It was Richard in a florist's truck and a little jacket with a logo on it. *Holy crap*, she thought. Fortunately, Richard did not see her. She was driving the old Prius today, not the Porsche. Freddie drove around the block to give Richard time to leave the area and then pulled back in the drive. She had been careful to watch the delivery truck and make sure he actually left and had not set up somewhere to watch the house. She thought to herself that she must be getting paranoid.

At the house, she found a really nice bouquet of roses, which Freddie quickly brought inside. She wanted no trace of anything. She fed them into the garbage disposal one by one to get rid of the evidence. The card, which she did not even read, along with the ribbons and cellophane went into the vase, which was then stuffed into a plastic bag. Freddie changed into blue jeans, tossed the bag in the Prius, and headed back to the office. In the parking lot, the bag went into the dumpster. The only thing she had forgotten was to eat lunch herself.

"Did you get lunch?" she asked Noah from the phone in her car.

"I got something from the deli," he replied. Freddie was off the hook on that account.

"Okay. I'll be back in a few minutes. Bye," Freddie said and hung up. She decided to just sit in the car for a moment to regain her composure. Instead, the quiet time gave her subconscious mind time to give her more things to worry about. The result was that before heading back into the office, she decided to call Angelique. She realized that she was really pissed at Jenny and owed Angelique a thank-you for alerting her to the mistake so was able to calm herself a bit before she called. She also knew that she needed to shoulder some of the blame because she had told the agency that she was single. She thanked Angelique and asked her to let Jenny know not to do that again. Then she told Angelique about Richard being the delivery boy. Angelique was shocked. She immediately realized the potential danger if Richard had bad intentions. Their agency was supposed to protect the client until the client was ready to share phone numbers and addresses. If Richard was a burglar, or worse, the agency would be liable. Of course, Angelique cared about Freddie's well-being too.

Finally, Freddie asked how Bob might have gotten the idea that he was going to get laid. As she went inside after hanging up, she could still hear Angelique's laughter and her words: "He said it was something you did with a lime, some salt, and sucking on your finger."

12

Randall J. Hunter

Randall J. Hunter sat at home alone. Again. He was a smart man, but the answer to his latest problem had eluded him for quite a while. Lately, he was really starting to grasp at straws. The most frustrating part was that he was not used to being at a loss for answers. RJ, as his friends called him, was a born problem solver. One of his earliest memories was about solving a problem. He could not have been more than five or six years old at the time. He and his older brother and sister were visiting his grandparents who had a small farm in Kansas. Well, Grandpa woke them up one morning asking for help rounding up a young lamb that had gotten loose. The plan was to surround the lamb and then Grandpa would tackle him. Well, the lamb was about as large as RJ, so he bolted between the outstretched arms of RJ and his brother. RJ went and got small tree branches to make it seem like the hands at the ends of his arms were larger. The next time they had her cornered, the lamb was more hesitant to bolt and was captured.

A few summers later, his brother had locked him in the corn crib, which is what older brothers do. RJ had pleaded to be let out, but his brother refused. So he studied the problem for a moment and began climbing. The walls of the corn crib were made of slats to let the air through, and the slats made a perfect ladder. Up over the top he went and down the outside.

Of course, this creative trait also got him into trouble. One summer, he was playing in the creek with a little wooden boat he had carved and decided he needed a lake, not a river. So he built a dam that flooded the cornfield and ruined about a quarter acre of crop before Grandpa found it and removed it.

His inquisitive nature had served him well once he learned how to control it. His problem today was that he was turning fifty in two weeks and was single with no prospects. He ticked off his good points. He was probably in the best health he had been in since the day after boot camp ended. He was nice looking, but not what one would call Calvin Klein handsome. He had a nice job as a research scientist at a private university. He had been studying the physics of how sound and light moved in water under a contract for the Navy.

Over the past year, he had tried to get back into the dating game. He'd been sidelined for seven years before that. He wasn't interested. His marriage had ended, and ended very badly almost fifteen years earlier. He dabbled in the normal routine of trying to meet someone new, but it had always fizzled. There were lots of women interested in him. That wasn't the problem. It was the type of woman he seemed to attract that was driving him nuts. Maybe it was his degree, or his position, or something that was just wrong with him, he told himself, but it seemed that the woman he met during these years were only interested in how he would make their life better. There was no emotion, no love, or even an interest in developing anything like that. The women he met wanted random sex or a meal ticket. He even started going back to church for a while hoping to meet someone there who had a different idea of what a relationship should be.

That hadn't worked and he had given up for a while. Now he was ready to try again. The problem was that he couldn't find an entry point. It wasn't the same as when he was in his twenties.

There were no friends with single sisters or cousins. Dating in the workplace was so politically incorrect that people were hesitant to share anything personal, much less a drink after work. That probably wouldn't have mattered anyway since his work hours were quite unconventional. There was no five o'clock whistle in the physics lab. In fact, the main lab he worked in was docked in the channel behind the parking lot of the research building. It was a 110-foot long converted trawler that had been outfitted with all kinds of special equipment for his work. It even had a minisubmarine, which he used to test his sound and light experiments. Just last week, he had taken her out for a sound test. He had coated the sub with a material made of soft foam, which was then covered with a rubberized paint. When a sonar unit sent out a ping, the sound wave was partially absorbed by the foam and partially shifted in its tone so the receiver never got a return signal. To the sonar operator on the ship, the sub just wasn't there.

The bottom line was that RJ wanted to be in a relationship but could not figure out how to meet anyone. Picking up girls in bars was out of the question. He had tried Internet dating with very bad results. Then he found an advertisement for the Sun 'n' Fun dating service in a weekend newspaper. The service the agency provided was to filter out the unsuitable people that used the online services and attempt to put two people together with a more personal touch.

Earlier in the week, RJ had called the agency and had his first interview. There was paperwork to fill out, but it was the interview that convinced him this might be a good way to go. The key was that the lady at the service, Angelique, actually met with him. She spent an hour with him having what seemed like a casual conversation. So when he put down that he was six-foot-two inches tall with a muscular build and short sandy hair, Angelique knew that to be true. From this, he knew that when he went to meet a woman, she would actually match the description that he was given. The down side was that the service was pricey; fifteen hundred dollars for a one-year subscription and a guarantee of at least three dates a month.

RJ had plunked down the cash partly because he was at a loss about what to do next and partly because he viewed it as an experiment. Of course, as a scientist, he liked experimentation. This thought reminded him of another aspect of his character that he probably needed to tell Angelique about the next time they met. One of the largest problems he had ever had to solve was his choice of career paths. He had been fascinated with science and mathematics ever since he could remember. Once, back on the farm, he had sat and watched a little garden snake glide effortlessly through the cornfield. He was a sneaky little kid and was able to keep close enough to it to watch it for almost thirty minutes. For months afterward, he wondered how a snake with no legs could do that. Of course, the Internet had not been invented yet, and he was in Kansas on a farm, so he had to wait until he got home to Jefferson City before he could get to the library and look up snakes in the encyclopedia. He didn't understand everything he read about it, but he had figured out that it was physics that made it work. This event probably got him started with getting to know the physical world. RJ's choice to study physics would have been pretty clear if he had not kept seeing it at work in other places. The way a bird flies and what makes a fish able to swim were certainly the result of applied physics, but the fact that nature, through evolution, had been able to apply the physics got him interested in biology. Then there was chemistry. He had learned that the fish needed that slimy surface to reduce drag. Of course, fish slime is a biochemical product, but the resulting reduction in drag was physics. Eventually, he just picked physics, but he never lost interest in the other sciences. Today's experiment was in human behavior and human interpersonal relations and dynamics.

Well, that was how he justified spending the money. The truth was that he was lonely and while he had male friends, he was always the one without a girlfriend or wife. He also recognized that there is a fundamental difference in having male friends and having a female friend. That difference is not about the sexual component at all, and RJ knew it. The difference was just a difference in perspective and in what it meant to be spiritually close to someone.

All these thoughts ran around in the back of his mind at the same time that his conscious mind was absorbing *Broca's Brain*. Carl Sagan was not a biologist. He was an astrophysicist. Still, he and RJ shared a broadly inquisitive mind. Both of these activities were interrupted by a soft beeping sound. It was regular but muffled. RJ drew himself out of the book and tuned it in. Once he had done so, he recognized it as the beeper on his telephone indicating he had a message. He walked to the phone and realized that he had closed the door to his home study earlier and that had muffled the sound.

He pressed the button. "You have one message. Message one was received at 3:45 PM today."

"Hi, RJ. This is Angelique with the service. I think I have a date for you. Please call me back and let me know if you are available this coming Saturday evening. Her name is Winifred, but she prefers to be called Freddie. She is tall and slender. Forty years old. She is a single mom who works as a receptionist, but she in college now. I was trying to find someone for you with an advanced degree, but since there was no one available, I thought you might like to meet her."

RJ clicked the delete button but did make a mental note to call in the morning.

He then retired to his study; found his overstuffed reading chair, his book, and a glass of rum; and settled in for the evening. Reading Michener's *The Covenant* had been enjoyable over the past few weeks, but tonight, in the back of his mind, there were random thoughts of what events might result from the call he would make in the morning.

13

Friday with R. J. Hunter

"Good morning. This is Angelique."

"Hi. This is RJ Hunter returning your call."

Angelique got all bubbly, saying, "Oh, good morning! I was hoping you would call! Freddie is really nice, and I am sure you will like her. I know she is younger than you are, but I don't think that will be a problem, do you?" Without waiting for a reply, she continued, "You don't turn fifty until next week, right?"

"Uh, yes, that's correct. Next week." RJ was quite a bit more subdued than Angelique. "I need to tell you something, though. There is no need to try and find a woman with an advanced degree, or even a degree at all. I am not an intelli-snob. In fact, the only reason I have an advanced degree is because I was more curious than I was conscientious about having a good job. After all, not many people get a degree in physics for the money. In fact, the smartest and best botanist I know has a high school diploma. Now, I am not saying to choose someone who would have trouble playing checkers with a monkey, but don't let a degree get in the way."

"I understand," Angelique said. "I can make arrangements for you at the Roadhouse if you like. Have you ever been there? Wait, I am ahead of myself. Are you free Saturday?"

"I like the Roadhouse. I've been there several times, but mostly for takeout. I really hate eating alone in a restaurant. And yes, Saturday is fine. Is this confirmed or do you need to call me back?"

Angelique said she would need to check with Freddie and would call with a time. "What will you wear? I need to tell her how to recognize you."

RJ was not used to planning what he would wear more than twenty-four minutes in advance much less twenty-four hours, so he stumbled a bit before deciding that he would wear a tan jacket and blue jeans.

14

Friday with Freddie

Friday morning was a pretty normal one for Freddie. She and Noah took separate cars to the office because he had a meeting downtown later that afternoon, and she had to pick up Brea from school. She didn't have plans with the agency tonight and was hoping to make it a special evening for her and Noah. On the way to the office, her cell phone rang. She looked at the screen pad. It was Angelique. *Oh no,* she thought. I don't want a date tonight. She considered not answering but decided she always had the ability to refuse and so took the call.

"Good morning! It's Angelique from the service." Freddie thought that apparently no one had ever told Angelique about caller ID and said, "I thought it was going to be you. What's up?"

"I have a new guy for you, if you are interested."

Freddie interrupted. "Sure, as long as it isn't tonight. I already have plans."

"Perfect! How about tomorrow at the Roadhouse? His name is Randall, but he goes by his initials, RJ. He is tall, nice looking, and in good physical condition. And the best part is that he is not over fifty years old" She said with a bit of a chuckle. "He's well educated. In fact, he has a PhD in experimental physics. I think you two would get along just great!"

Sometimes Angelique's effervescence could be really annoying, but Freddie realized that it was all part of the job. "That sounds nice. How about telling him six thirty? What will he be wearing?"

Freddie shuddered as she heard Angelique's reply. "A sport coat and blue jeans. The coat will be tan." Freddie's mind free-associated this with what Richard had worn, and she had not liked him at all. She accepted the date, and as she continued her drive to the office, she called the sitter to make arrangements for the evening. It would be a late night, so she got Sarah's mom to agree to let Brea stay over.

Once at the office, she found that Noah was already in a conference call, so she couldn't just poke her head in the office and tell him about her plans. Instead, she got into the calendar on the computer and opened up Noah's day planner. His afternoon meeting was scheduled to end at five o'clock so she made a new entry at five thirty. It said: "Rush home—dinner, late movie, and maybe more, with Freddie." A few minutes later, the little icon popped up that said Noah had accepted the appointment, and a little smiley face had been added.

Friday night was Freddie's way of thanking Noah for his patience with her studies. Even if it was thin, she did acknowledge that it was there. She was very aware of the fact that he didn't like her being gone so much. To compensate, she had gone out of her way on several occasions to make sure he knew that she appreciated it. Tonight would be dinner and a bang-bang, shoot-'em-up movie, which was the kind she hated and Noah liked. She had been pretty careful to pick a restaurant that was not one of the ones where she had gone on a date. The last thing she needed was for a waiter to recognize her. No, she corrected herself, the last thing she needed was to actually run into one of her dates while she was out with Noah. The theater was right next door, and it was in a dinner theatre style where you sat at a table instead of in row seating. They could have snacks and a drink with the movie.

The day went by quickly but uneventfully. Freddie and Noah barely had time to say hello to each other. He finished his conference call, bolted out the door for a lunch meeting with a defense contractor, and only returned to get his messages and his folder for his afternoon meeting. She spent the day working on the budget, accounts receivable, and a new marketing initiative. At least, she told herself, the latter was interesting and taxed her creativity and skills. She resolved that it was time to hire an accountant or bookkeeper so that she could focus full time on the marketing and her studies. She figured she'd be done in another three months and was eager to finish. After she finished her degree, she planned on hiring a new receptionist and spending all her time in marketing. Any leftover time would be spent with Brea. She knew she needed to make sure she had that extra time because she remembered what it had been like turning eleven. Teenage America was not a picnic for a girl in public school. Freddie resolved to be as available as she possibly could be just in case Brea needed her. She was their only child, and she needed both a mother and a best friend.

The need for a combined relationship of friend and mother was not a new revelation for Freddie. She recalled a time when Brea was about two. Freddie and Noah were not going to have any more children. Brea was a blessing, but she had come with a price. Complications had assured Freddie that Brea would be an only child. Playing on the floor with Brea, Freddie realized that, unlike her childhood, Brea would have no one to play with unless Freddie filled that role. She also realized that she could not sacrifice her authority as parent. She had walked a tightrope between authority and pal for the past ten years and was looking forward to at least another eight. The reward, though, was clear.

As Brea grew, Freddie would be able to change from authority figure to advisor, and eventually to friend. Her goal was that when Brea was an adult, Brea would be her best buddy.

Freddie had orchestrated the day in her mind over and over again. She was going to give Noah the time of his life. She timed everything perfectly, arranged for Brea to stay at Sarah's, laid out her clothing in her mind, and had allowed time for a drink or two before they even left the house for the show.

As she had planned, Freddie arrived home before Noah. She had left the office a little bit after three in order to pick up Brea from school and drop her off at Sarah's. At home, she scrubbed the day off of her face and went about creating the goddess that only subdued makeup, great hair, and a tight, black dress on a well-exercised body could accomplish. By the time Noah was expected, she was ready for anything and had more than a few things in mind.

"You're late," she said to Noah as he walked in. She saw his eyes run over her, and she could tell by the look he gave her that she had been successful in her preparations. He wanted her right then and there. "Too bad," she continued. If you had been here a half hour ago we would have had some time to kill." She gave him that dirty little smile that had first attracted his attention back in college and walked out the door to the car.

Dinner was light and heavily accented by the glances and sometimes outright stares of other men in the restaurant. Freddie took a particular pride in knowing this was happening, and Noah echoed the feeling in knowing that those guys knew he was taking her home, not them. It was sort of the male ego's version of that old Kennel Ration commercial: "My girl's better than your girl, my girl's better than yours..." The theatre seating in the movie house was composed of single rows of tables, each raised above the one below by about two feet. The arrangement was like bleachers at the ball game, but each table had a curved and padded bench-style seat, making it more like a booth. Small candles on the tables gave enough light to find a chip and the dip if you needed it. There was a small button that served to light a waitress call light at the edge of the table. It was like the ones in airplanes, but dim. The layout was such that the people next to you could not see you because of the curve of the booth and the people behind you were blocked by their own table and the short wall along the walkway. Sitting in the booth, a couple may as well have been alone. It was the perfect place for a man and woman to experience just enough intimacy to ramp things up for later and not quite enough to get them into trouble. And of course, there was tequila for her and wine for him. Judging from the remainder of the evening after they had returned home, they both considered it to have been a good investment, even if for different reasons. Freddie had expressed her thanks and Noah had been remotivated to be patient.

15

Saturday Morning

Saturday morning brought rays of sunshine into the bedroom through tiny slits in the blinds, giving the whole room a pinstriped look. Freddie slid out of bed and headed to the kitchen. Along the way, she followed a trail of debris, picking up her bra, panties, Noah's trousers, socks, shirt, and finally her dress. All of that, except the dress, went into the hamper. The dress, of course, was dry-clean only. In the kitchen, she started the coffeepot then headed to the showers, where her subconscious mind reminded her of a lecture in class sometime last year. She thought that last night, while entertaining and fun, had achieved the desired goals but might still have been somewhat Pavlovian. The thought was troubling, but she decided she was overthinking things and put it aside.

Noah woke up as Brea bounced into the room and jumped on the bed. Sarah's mom had dropped her off just after breakfast, and she had let herself in. "Did you have a good time at the movie?" she asked.

"I had a great time, girl. Did you have fun with Sarah?" he responded.

"Yes, I did." Brea beamed. "We played catch in the yard and then took her dog to the dog park."

"Breakfast is ready," Freddie called, and Brea scurried out of the room, which was fortunate because it gave Noah time to find something to put on before he got up.

"I already ate," Brea informed her mother.

"Well, then you can just sit and have a cup of juice with us." Freddie replied with a smile and a pat on her head. Freddie put pancakes and sausage on two plates and served up two hot coffees and a glass of artificially flavored, artificially fortified, artificially sweetened red liquid that Brea called juice. "You know, sweetie, you really are going to need to read the label on that stuff and find something else to drink pretty soon. If you don't, all your hair will fall out, and your eyes will roll back in your head and stay that way forever."

Brea rolled her eyes at this, and Freddie did not miss the opportunity. "See, there go the eyes now!"

Noah was plowing through his breakfast. Apparently he had managed to work up an appetite since dinner last night.

"Hungry, dear?" Freddie teased him.

"Actually, yes. And I am looking forward to a big lunch, too, if you have the time to help me burn off the breakfast," he shot back.

Freddie burned a hole in his head with her stare. He knew she was concerned that soon their little Brea would not miss the innuendo and that he should behave.

"We'll see," she said. "I need to put in the laundry and do some dusting. The tile needs a wipe down too."

Noah looked at her quizzically. Freddie clarified her implication saying "If you help me with my chores, I would have time to help you with yours."

Noah just said, "I'm not very good at that stuff. Maybe Brea could help. I need to get the paper and read the new engineering journal anyway."

Unbelievable, Freddie thought to herself. He was willing to give up an encore performance rather than wipe down some tile. She let it roll off, though. She was used to it. Instead, she looked at Brea and asked "So, kiddo, you up to helping with the laundry?"

With an impish grin, Brea said, "Yes. And I can start right now." Holding up Noah's boxers, she added, "Look what I found under the table."

Freddie and Brea both laughed while Noah turned a bit pink around the ears. "Come on. Let's get started. I have an interview this evening, and I need to get all this done before I go," Freddie said. She and Brea began clearing the table while Noah began the process of developing a full-blown blue funk. "Don't worry, honey, I will make dinner before I leave," Freddie added as she began washing the dishes.

The rest of the day was filled with housework for Freddie, homework for Brea, and golf for Noah. Around 4:00 PM, Freddie put together a meal of potatoes, coleslaw, and pulled pork in barbeque sauce. Brea did what she could, and in keeping with Freddie's parenting plan, Freddie let her do almost everything she was capable of doing. Most importantly, she had Brea read directions from the *Joy of Cooking*. This was more to exercise Brea's reading skills and her ability to follow instructions than any help Freddie needed with the recipe. Once complete, the coleslaw went in the refrigerator and the potatoes and pork went in the oven. Freddie showed Brea how to set the temperature to warm. The timer was set so that a loud buzzer would go off and Brea was instructed again in the use of hot pads. Freddie told her she could turn the oven off, unless Noah decided to use a top burner for something and then he would need to take care of it. Freddie had no delusions about Noah using the stove but had used the moment to reinforce Brea's understanding of safety around stovetops.

Noah came in from the golf course while Freddie was getting dressed. The Roadhouse was a little bit country in ambience so Freddie put on a white shirt, blue jeans, and her boots. She thought she would look good and not clash with Mr. Tan Jacket and Jeans. *What was his name?* she thought. *JR?* She shook her head. That was the guy from the television show. He was "RJ." That was it. "RJ Hunter." She wondered if she were going to meet a refuge from the Duck Dynasty but then remembered that the guy had a doctorate in something. "Physics," she remembered and said out loud if under her breath in an attempt to make the memory stick. Her last problem was where to stick her recorder. These jeans were a bit tight, and her shirt was one of those fitted ones country girls wore. The cut was "rodeo style" and made for ladies wanting to look a little bit cowboy, but wanting to make sure everyone knew how the deck was stacked. Finally, she figured out that if she put the recorder in her boot and ran the microphone wire up the inside of her blue jeans, she could position it right next to her belt buckle and no one would notice.

16

Dinner with R. J. Hunter

While still in her car in the parking lot, Freddie reached into her boot to turn on the recorder. She had taken the Porsche just because it made her feel good. Well, better than the Prius did anyway. Looking at the door of the Roadhouse, she saw a man whom she took to be RJ. He was trim but certainly not skinny. His tan blazer and jeans gave him a more rugged look than the one Richard had managed. The difference was probably that she associated a blue blazer and jeans with a preppie and a tan jacket and jeans with Marshal Dillon. He had close cropped dark hair with a fair amount of salt around the sides. What struck her most was his posture. He stood straight as an arrow without looking stiff. His posture and carriage served to make him look even taller. She decided this was probably her date and lifted herself out of the Porsche. He spotted her before she had a chance to close the door. His look was so direct that she wondered if someone at the agency hadn't given him a description of what she was wearing. *Impossible*, she thought. *I hadn't decided myself until a while ago.*

Freddie decided the best way to deal with this was to meet his stare straight on and so she walked toward the building locked onto his gaze. "Are you RJ?" she asked as she neared. "Yes, ma'am," he said as he stuck out his hand. "And you are Freddie, I presume?"

"Nice to meet you, RJ. I didn't think you needed to presume anything. The way you were looking at me, I thought you knew who I was."

"No, ma'am." He grinned. "Just wishful thinkin'." He almost smiled, but it came out as a sort of half stifled grin. Freddie smiled back, thinking that she liked this guy already.

Inside, the air was thick with the smell of beer, beef, and barbeque sauce. The Roadhouse was one of those places with peanut shells on the floor, closely packed seating, and country music for background atmosphere. It even had a little dance floor for boot scootin'. RJ looked at her, took a sniff, and said, "They should make perfume out of that stuff. There's no better way to catch a man than to smell like stuff he likes. You know, baseball gloves, tool boxes, hot engine grease, horses. That would make a man feel much more comfortable than all that flowery stuff."

Freddie looked a bit stunned as she examined his face. *Was he serious?* she thought.

He busted a grin and said, "Too soon for the jokes?"

Laughing lightly, he continued, "Sorry about that, but when I was told to meet you here, I just sort of fell into character." He continued, "Let's get a table and a proper introduction."

Freddie's attraction to RJ was immediate. It was also completely unexplainable. RJ was admittedly rock solid and handsome. The way he stood and walked was nothing less than authoritative, but there was nothing superior about it. He was just charismatic. His self-assurance or self-confidence was quite evident but not demeaning. He was the kind of guy that people just knew could handle himself in whatever situation might arise. The grins he had already shared with her were wide and genuine. His eyes had an impish sparkle in them that promised many laughs. All of this is what made her attraction to him unexplainable. These same traits in other men had always been harbingers of absolute arrogance. Freddie recognized them and had prepared herself to feel small and insignificant. The feeling never came.

She lightly tapped the face of the microphone with her fingernail twice. When she played it back later, these two little ticks would remind her to recapture what was going on in her head. It was a little trick she had developed to remind herself that something important had happened and she was not able to jot it down.

Crunching their way to a table through a sea of peanut shells on the floor, they were seated in a booth near the back of the place. Kalie, the waitress, seated them, and then using a crayon, she wrote her name upside down on the paper table cloth. "Can I start you off with something to drink?"

RJ deferred to Freddie, as any gentleman would do. "Tequila, please. Whatever you have that is reposado." Freddie knew a place like this was not likely to have the higher quality product but did hope for something with some flavor. Kalie looked at RJ.

"That sounds good. Do you have Mescal?" RJ inquired.

Kalie nodded and went off to fetch the drinks while Freddie and RJ opened up the menus in accordance with the ritual of date dining. There was the usual banter of "What are you getting?" and "Do you want an appetizer?" but it wasn't stiff or forced. It was just wasting time until the tequila came. Both of them knew that as soon as they actually started a conversation, Kalie would be back and interrupt them.

Kalie returned and took their order. RJ ordered a full rack of ribs. Freddie ordered a steak, with a potato and broccoli. Each of them thought that a good appetite was a good sign when neither of them was overweight in the slightest. Each of them deduced that the other must have a high activity level in order to sustain such a diet and remain fit and trim.

Taking their shot glasses in hand, they looked into each other's eyes for the first time since RJ's opening joke. He noticed that hers were the dark brown kind with little yellow highlights around the edges. They reminded him of the Caribbean islands for some unknown reason. He enjoyed their depth and sensed that they had lots of stories to tell. She found herself wandering around in his speckled, dark blue eyes like a butterfly in a meadow. She too felt that there was a lot going on in there. She blinked, breaking the trance that had snuck up on both of them. He raised his glass with a broad grin. "To meeting new people."

The moment was broken, but certainly not lost on either one of them.

Her date with RJ was completely abnormal if normal could be defined by her dates up to this point. Since she started her project, Freddie had dated twenty different men. RJ was number twenty-one. Her goal was twenty-five. RJ was somehow different than the others. As the evening went by, she found herself wondering what it was about this guy that was so unusual. Sure, he had a Ph.D. So did numbers 10 and 14. Number 9 had a master's degree in party planning. That was a story all by itself. RJ was polite, but so were most of her dates, except for that idiot Jake. One thing she noticed was that RJ's eyes were never still. He always had a scan going, but it was subtle. After observing him for a bit, she knew that he was aware of every person in the room, what they were doing, eating, drinking, and whether any particular couple was having a nice time or not. He did all this without seeming for a moment to not be paying attention to her. Another thing that she acknowledged, even though she resisted it for quite some time, was that she was simply comfortable with him. There was no pressure to be the date he expected, and he was clearly not trying to impress her beyond just sharing the evening. She felt the protective barriers she had erected start to weaken. The barriers were necessary for the project, and she worked hard to keep them in place, but it was not easy with RJ. It wasn't easy simply because she didn't feel they were necessary.

RJ had decided that he liked Freddie. He didn't really have a reason why. He didn't really feel that he needed one. She was obviously not telling him complete stories during their conversation, but he also got the impression that she wasn't really lying. She just seemed to be leaving things out. He concluded that she, like he, probably had suffered through some difficult experiences in her past, and she was just letting this first date play itself out. She could always call Angelique if she wanted to see him again. So he resolved to just enjoy the conversation, the food, and the company of a lovely woman. If nothing else came of it, then at least he had a nice night. From the looks of things, she was having a good time as well. It was nothing spectacular. It was just pleasant.

At the end of the evening, Freddie said something to RJ she had not said to any of her previous dates. "I'd really like to do this again, if you don't mind." It had been her policy up until now that the man would need to want a second date. It was actually integral to her project that this rule be in place. As she cursed herself for saying it, she realized that she really had not been able to stop it. It just came out.

RJ had just smiled and said that he enjoyed the evening and that he would call the service. Then he walked her to her car, held the door for her, and stood there in the lot watching her drive off.

On the way home, Freddie reflected on the evening. Her feeling of simply being comfortable around RJ was quite overwhelming, and she realized she had not felt that way in a long time. Her job was an act. She wondered if her marriage was an act as well. She had just gotten so used to the character she played that she had not realized it. She did know that she felt perfectly comfortable as Brea's mom, so that was not an act. That was real. She determined then and there that her new goal would be to do whatever she needed to do so that she and Noah could have that level of comfort. She wanted to feel that closeness with her husband.

She also realized that she felt comfortable with RJ even though she had spent most of the evening skirting the truth. There was only one outright lie. Somewhere in the evening, she had said she was divorced. It was the only way to tell RJ about Brea, and she had wanted to share with him her joy of being Brea's mom.

RJ got home from his date with Freddie and began packing his bag. He would be leaving in the morning on a three-week research cruise. All the equipment had been already packed and loaded by a crew of graduate students and deck hands. He just needed a duffel bag with a couple changes of clothing, personal items, and his laptop. At four thirty the next morning, he walked out of the house, drove to the dock, and boarded the ship.

17

Sunday

The service hadn't called all week, and Freddie was able to spend her evenings with her husband and daughter. Part of her had wished that Angelique would call with another date with RJ, but the bigger part had been focused on trying to develop a closeness with her husband Noah that was similar to what she had felt with RJ. As the week went by, she realized that Noah had never made her feel as comfortable as RJ had, even when they were in college. Still, she did her best. After all, she told herself, she had made a commitment and needed to do her best to live up to it. She needed this for Brea, for Noah and, if nothing else, to preserve her own self-respect. Nonetheless, Freddie also started to wonder if Noah had ever felt really comfortable with her. She even managed to bring this up during one late-night conversation. Noah had claimed that he did. During her semi-meditative state in the shower, though, she often still would get the feeling that he was more complacent with her as his wife than he was comfortable with her as a partner. Whatever it was she had felt with RJ, it was on a different plane than any emotion she had ever felt with Noah. Earlier in the week, she had determined to find out if she could find this kind of a relationship with the man she had loved since college.

By Sunday morning, having spent every night together, much of which was spent in casual conversation, Freddie had a little bit different perspective. First, she noticed that Noah really didn't want the conversation as much as he wanted to watch his television shows or read his engineering magazines. Freddie had steered their conversations so that they had eventually covered all aspects of their life. Noah loved Brea. That was certain. He would do anything for her, unless he was busy and whatever she wanted to do didn't seem important to him. But for the really important things, Freddie knew that he would not let her down. Of course a forty-one-year-old engineer and a ten-year-old girl often have different definitions of what is important, but that distinction was lost on Noah.

They talked about her master's degree. She brought the conversation around to how much it meant to her and how much she was enjoying the work needed to get it. Somewhere in that conversation, though, Freddie realized that Noah's apparent patience with her was not patience at all. It was in these conversations that his answers and comments became very brief, sometimes being reduced to just one word. Freddie noticed that he would often change the subject rather than pursue a point. He never actually asked her a question about the topic. She finally realized that what she had taken for patience was actually just disinterest.

Richard had been working on his next move for a week. He had carefully selected Freddie from the girls the service had offered him, and he was pleased when she not only drove up in a Porsche but was nice looking as well. Because she was working as a receptionist, he presumed that she had poorly developed job skills, even though the agency said she had some sort of liberal arts degree. His ruse with the flower delivery was born of opportunity, not planning. His consulting had not been going well, and he was working part-time as a delivery man. After his date with Freddie, he figured out that he might be able to deliver flowers to the agency, hoping to get her home address from them. He used the premise that the flowers would go bad if he didn't deliver them. That had worked well enough. Freddie's home was in a wealthy neighborhood in Weston, a small community west of Ft. Lauderdale, and the house was easily worth a half a million. That added to the Porsche solidified his intentions for Freddie. She was an unskilled, wealthy, single mom, nearing forty, and she was in need of companionship. She was perfect.

Once Richard had her home address, he was able to go online and, for a small fee, use the reverse lookup service and get her home phone number. His problem was what to do next. He thought about dropping by and surprising her but rejected that idea because it would quickly become apparent that he had gotten her home address through means that most law enforcement officers would consider to be stalking. He could just call, but that resulted in the same problem. How would he explain how he got her number? He considered using the delivery truck to cruise the neighborhood and find the closest park. Parks are good places for moms to take their kids, and Freddie was transparent in how much she cared for he daughter. If he found the park, he could pick a spot and watch it until the two of them showed up. He might be able to create a chance encounter. He rejected that idea too because that really was stalking, and the last thing he needed was any problems with the law. Of course, he could always just go back to the agency and ask Angelique to arrange a second date. That option was easy, but it seemed to lack the splash he wanted. He was stumped. When he finally admitted that to himself, he called Angelique.

When Angelique called, Freddie saw who it was on the caller ID. She found herself hoping that the call would be to set up the next date with RJ. When Angelique said Richard's name, though, she accepted because Richard was part of the project and completing that was extremely important. She wanted to ask if RJ had called, but resisted. During the call, Angelique reminded Freddie of her pending date with Bob as well. Next Saturday, she was to meet Bob for date number three. Almost as an afterthought, Angelique asked how Freddie liked RJ.

Freddie was surprised and asked, "Didn't he call you afterward?"

Angelique said, "No. And that's odd because, as you know, our protocols are for the men to call in and let us know if they want a second date or not. I haven't heard anything."

Freddie was actually a bit hurt by this news, but she hid it well. She accepted the date with Richard for Wednesday and hung up. Angelique put down the receiver of her phone and leaned back in her chair, wondering what the hell was wrong with RJ that he wasn't interested in Freddie. She had thought they would be really good together. She was just about to make another call to another client when her computer emitted a sound like a gong.

An electronic voice came online and said, "Your spam filter is full. Please review e-mails tagged as spam. E-mails tagged in error may be recovered by unclicking the spam designator and moving them to the inbox." The recorded voice was accompanied by a popup window, which displayed the same message.

Being a dutiful slave to the mandates of her computer-driven world, Angelique opened her spam filter and looked at the long list of junk. Her mouse hovered over the "delete all" button as she scanned down the subject lines. There was no way she was going to review one thousand e-mails. The subject lines were all the same. "Buy This Now!" "There's a home invasion every ten seconds." "What you need to know about home heating." "Elect Joey to Congress." "Freddie."

Wait! That one! She looked at the last e-mail. It was from DrR@RVDeepview.org. "DrR? Could that be Dr. Randall?" She remembered from watching the National Geographic Channel that RV was often used to designate a research vessel. She deselected the spam icon and moved it to her inbox.

The message read:

> Angelique, Please tell Freddie that I had a very nice evening. I am now at sea doing some research and will be back in three weeks. Let her know that I would like to see her again when I return.
>
> V/R RJ Hunter

Angelique typed in a reply.

> Dr. Hunter. Good to hear from you. I apologize for the late reply, but it seems that your e-mail was somehow routed to the spam filter. I will make sure you are tagged as "friendly" to prevent this from happening again. I will pass your message on to Freddie and arrange something for two weeks from this coming Saturday. If you are delayed, please let me know.
>
> Sincerely,
Angelique

She pressed "Send" and started to call Freddie back but decided she needed to deal with other girls first. Freddie was set for her next two dates, and that ought to be enough for now. She completely overlooked the fact that she had not forwarded RJ's e-mail and had now failed to let Freddie know that he had contacted her.

At the same time that Angelique had hung up her phone, Freddie had disconnected as well. Noah looked up from his paper and asked, "Who was that?"

"I have another interview for Saturday. So this week, I have no class on Monday, just Wednesday and an interview," Freddie told Noah. "I'll put them on the calendar so you can keep track easily."

Freddie still wanted to put Noah's mind at ease and searched for something to say. Remembering that RJ was number twenty-one, she did the math quickly in her head. One more date with Bob. Two more dates with RJ, plus two dates with Richard made five, plus four new guys at three dates each made twelve for a grand total of seventeen. "I have about seventeen more interviews to do, and then I will be all finished. It won't be long."

Noah looked at her again. She didn't like the expression on his face at all. Something was bothering him and bothering him a lot. She had hoped to ease things, but apparently, her comment had had the opposite effect.

"What's wrong?" she asked. "I thought you would be happy."

His frown was not deep or angry, but it was stern. "I just wonder what will happen after you get this degree. You having a master's degree is going to change everything, isn't it? When you started taking classes, I thought it was a whim. I thought you were on a lark, just going to classes for a change of pace or to get back into your reading hobby." Noah realized the error in his choice of words immediately, and added, "Sorry. I mean your literature."

"Whatever do you mean, honey?" Freddie was genuinely confused.

Noah continued, and it all spilled out uncontrollably. Everything he had held back was put on the table. "You're going to get this degree and then what? Are you going to be happy with your job as the receptionist? You're going to want to put those letters after your name, right? And I suspect you will want to put them to use." Noah paused to catch his breath. He was uncorking two years of slowly building concern. "What does that do to my business? What does that do to my business model? I won't be able to have you as my receptionist any more, can I? No! You're not going to be Freddie, my hot and perky receptionist. You're going to be Winifred B. Kazlowski, MS. What are you trying to do to me?"

"Brea," Freddie called. "How would you like to go to the park for a while? Get your ball glove and meet me at the car, sweetie." Freddie was too stunned by Noah's outburst to even begin to formulate a reply. She hated fighting and arguing. During the years they had been married, she would often let Noah have his way just to avoid the conflict. After what he had just said, she needed to think. Noah went back to his magazine while Freddie got her keys.

Brea tossed her ball and glove into the Porsche and hopped in beside her mom. "I was hoping to go to the park today. How did you know?"

Freddie smiled at her daughter and said, "Just a lucky guess, I suppose."

At the park, Brea and Freddie played catch for a while before some other kids showed up. Freddie suggested that Brea play catch with them. "I'm a little tired, honey. Would it be all right if I just sat on the bench and watched?"

Noah's choice of words became the focal point of her reflections. "My business," he had said. "My receptionist" and "My business model" were his exact words. Her interest in literature was a "reading hobby." It started to pile up. She remembered his complaint a week or so ago that the time she was spending on her classes and interviews was taking away from the time she had to do the laundry and go grocery shopping. Slowly, painfully, she saw her past fifteen years in a new light. It was a brighter light, and it hurt. Her place, in Noah's mind, was nothing more than an asset. She cooked and cleaned at home, and she was the final touch on the waiting room at the office. She existed solely for his benefit. Freddie thought that realizing this was the most painful experience she had ever had. She was wrong. As she continued to reflect on her life and the recent events in it, she became aware of the true source of Noah's anger. He was afraid that she was going to surpass him. In his world, a world where status is measured by credentials, she would have the higher degree. She would still be responsible for the office work, but she had already disclosed her hopes of hiring a bookkeeper and focusing on management and marketing. In Noah's mind, she was taking over his business. "His business." Saying it aloud brought her out of her almost trancelike state of reflection.

She watched Brea play with her friends for a while longer while she regained control of her emotions. Just when she thought she had it under control, she saw the florist's delivery truck cruise past the other side of the park. It was from the same florist as the one she had seen Richard driving. It was too far away to see if he was driving it today. She wondered if she should be afraid of Richard. Was he stalking her? Was he dangerous? Realizing that she simply didn't care at the moment, she got up and called to Brea, "Time to go home, sweetie."

That night, Freddie stayed in the guest bedroom. She told Noah she was not feeling well and didn't want to keep him awake if she tossed and turned in her sleep. He had often complained about how her nightmares kept him up. She didn't have them often, but now she realized that he had never asked her much about them. He hadn't really cared about her bad dreams or what was causing them. He had only cared that they had interrupted his own sleep. Freddie didn't sleep much that night. Everything that she thought was theirs, turned out to be his. At least that was how Noah saw things. Even Freddie herself was just a piece of property. By morning, though, she had resolved to stand up for herself and no longer subjugate her skills or her body to Noah's will. If he was willing to adjust, she would make the effort, too, but she would live her life on her terms.

18

Freddie's Law

Monday morning began routinely enough. Freddie got Brea ready for school and made breakfast. She dropped Brea off, and Noah took his own car to the office. When Freddie arrived, she went straight in to drafting and asked Jimmy to come out and man the phone for a while. Then Freddie went into Noah's office and shut the door.

"Noah. What you said yesterday is correct." He wanted to interject something, perhaps ask what was going on, but Freddie put up her hand. "Hear me out," she stated. It was not a question. Her years of avoiding arguments had not prepared him well for this new Freddie. He smugly sat back, thinking he would just watch the show and then take control of the situation.

"This is *your* company. It is *your* business. I have been a loyal employee, a good housekeeper, and a faithful wife. I have been a good mother to Brea, or at least I believe I have. I put my life into *your* business and *you* have been successful. I, on the other hand, have only been successful at making you successful. Yesterday, you made it clear that all this is yours, not ours. Today, I am going to define what is mine and not yours. My mind belongs to me. I will study what I want and for as long as I want. My body belongs to me. How much of it you get to see or enjoy is my decision. Whether my body sits at a reception desk or in a corner office is my choice. I do, however, grant that whether that corner office is in this building or in one owned by a new employer is your decision. Whether I do laundry or hire a maid will be my decision. I grant you that Brea is our daughter, but I am her mother, and I will decide how she develops as a young woman. You simply have no experience in being a young woman and your experience in parenting is limited. Now, if you can deal with me being a human being, a person, who is your equal, then we can focus on rebuilding our marriage on more equal footing. You will have some time to think about because I am taking the day off."

Noah started to say something, but she was already out the door. The thought in his mind was the same as when she started, "How can I retake control of the situation?"

Freddie got into the Porsche and headed out to Alligator Alley. That straight flat stretch of road was looking very therapeutic at the moment. She was no dummy, though. She knew there would be an occasional patrolman and didn't need to deal with getting pulled over. It took three miles of driving the speed limit, but eventually, she found what she was looking for. A cherry red Corvette with Michigan plates blew past her and a broad grin broke across her face. She let him get about three miles ahead of her and then she stomped it. The Porsche jumped ahead even though she was already doing seventy. The Corvette would trip any speed traps ahead, and she could just enjoy the rush. She backed off the accelerator when she hit a hundred miles per hour. It took about ten minutes, but eventually she had gained on the Corvette. When she was about a mile behind him, she was ready to back off again to gain some space. The guy in the 'vette, however, had apparently spotted her and wanted to play. He floored it and opened up some space between them. Freddie just kept it at one hundred miles per hour and enjoyed the ride. The Corvette was about two miles ahead of her when his brake lights came on, and he slowed quickly. Apparently, his radar detector had chirped. She slowed too, and before she caught up to him, she did a U-turn and headed back east toward Weston.

Freddie stopped for lunch at a small place with no name and then went to do some shopping. She did not want to go home, and it was too early to pick up Brea from school. She didn't buy anything. She just wandered around the mall. Inside the mall, she found a quiet bench near the food court and for a while just sat and watched people. Her mind wandered back to watching RJ watching people in the restaurant, and she began to appreciate this past time a bit more. Of course, it also fit in somewhat with her project, so she told herself she was not really wasting time altogether. By the time she finally picked up Brea from school, she had worked out the most significant issues in her mind. She would give it a go if Noah would.

At home, she found Noah's answer. Shortly after she had left the office, Noah had come home, packed his bag and his golf clubs, and left. There was a note on the kitchen table explaining things.

He wrote:

> I find it hard to believe that after all I have given you, this home, your car, your clothes, and the trips you made me take you on, that this is how you show your appreciation. Think about the damage you are doing to my business. You may need to start driving the Prius again. You can call me to come home when you start thinking about us instead of you-you-you. I called the temp service and I have a new receptionist so you don't need to come to work until you sort this out.

Freddie took the note and hid it before Brea could read it. The note had served to answer the questions she had about whether the marriage could be saved. She put it aside instead of tearing it up because she immediately knew that, if it came to that, her divorce lawyer would want to see it. It was evidence that Noah had abandoned her and the house. Brea had seen her reading it, however, and asked, "What's that?"

"Oh. It's a note from your daddy. He says he was called out of town on a business trip for a little while. It looks like it's just you and me, kiddo."

19

Outing Richard

Brea and Freddie had made the best of Tuesday. Brea's routine was nearly the same as any other day. Freddie's day, however, was somewhat of a roller coaster ride. She had called the office twice, and the new receptionist had refused to put her through to Noah. After making her wait for two hours, he did call Freddie. He didn't ask why she had called, and Freddie couldn't help but wonder if her reason had been something urgent, perhaps relating to Brea, how she could have contacted Noah. What Noah did ask was whether or not she was ready to apologize. When Freddie attempted to have a discussion, Noah simply hung up. He was freezing her out. She had seen him do this before. Once in college when he had a falling out with an old friend, he just stopped talking to the man. In business, he had to be more careful, but over the course of the years, she had seen two other contractors go on his list.

Freddie had to accept the fact that she had two choices. She could apologize and go back to being his waiting room trinket, or she could take control of her life. Twice more that day, she picked up the phone to dial his number. Twice more, she put it down in search of her decision. The third time she picked up the phone, she dialed Sarah's mom, Pauline. Arrangements were made for Brea to stay with Sarah when Freddie went out for her date with Richard on Wednesday.

It hadn't occurred to her before, but as she got dressed, she couldn't help but wonder if Noah hadn't decided to leave the house partly just to make it harder for her to go out on her interviews. She dismissed the thought, still wanting to give him the benefit of the doubt. She didn't want to think of him as being vindictive.

Before she left the house, Freddie reviewed her notes on Richard. To her dismay, she noticed the entry about the last moments of her last date when she had put her finger on his lips and said, "Next time." Now it was the next time, and she was a bit freaked out with the flowers and the delivery truck at the park. Freddie desperately wanted to dig into his background and see if he was some sort of known pervert, but couldn't. First of all, it was the agency's responsibility to make sure that her dates were all more or less normal. At the very least, she was not supposed to be dating any rapists who were on parole or awaiting trial. Secondly, if she dug into these men too early, it could influence the way the dates went and that would create problems with her project. She did put a can of mace in her bag, though. Just in case.

On their first date, Freddie may have overdone things with her attire, so tonight she chose a much more conservative outfit. It was a simple gray business suit. She was planning on telling him she had just come from the office. *Dumbass*, she thought to herself. Receptionists don't wear business suits. She took that off and put on a more stylish jacket. Sometimes it was hard keeping things straight. Finally, she looked like a receptionist, and she went and got into the Porsche. If she took the Prius, it would really look funny.

Richard was waiting for her at the bar at Chili's. He was actually having what looked like a pretty intimate discussion with another woman when she walked in, so she decided to sit on one of the little benches by the door. Her plan was to just watch him and pretend like she had not seen him. She checked to make sure her recorder was turned on, tapped the microphone twice to remind her of this interlude, and settled in. From all appearances, it was a classic boy-meets-girl moment with a happy exchange on names and, yes, phone numbers, until he finally checked his watch and glanced at the door. Freddie saw it coming and averted her eyes so that he did not see her looking. Richard saw Freddie waiting there. He thought he was in the clear because he didn't think she had seen him. He excused himself from his new friend and made his way to the hostess stand.

"Freddie!" he said in mock surprise. "What are you doing waiting here? You didn't come to find me?"

"Oh, hi, Richard," Freddie said. "I just got here a minute ago and thought I was here ahead of you. How've you been?"

"I've had a great week. Most of my meetings have been very productive. How have you been?"

Freddie figured that he was referring more to meetings like the one at the bar than to legitimate business meetings. But, she told herself, "Let this play out." She put on her sad face and said, "Honestly, Richard? It's been a horrible week. Let's get a drink and I'll tell you all about it."

Three minutes later, Freddie had put down her first shot of Tequila and played with the second one, running her lime-soaked finger around the rim of the glass as she stared into it. "I was let go from my job as a receptionist yesterday. Fired, after fifteen years of service." She almost added that she had even slept with the boss but decided better of it.

Richard didn't say anything. Either that or whatever he had said didn't register with Freddie. While Freddie had been watching Richard, she had also been remembering the details of their first date. She had even gotten the recording out earlier to make sure she remembered things correctly. Freddie had some suspicions about Richard's motivations, and now she was playing the few cards she held with the intent of drawing him out. Putting on her best sad face, she looked at Richard and said, "Would you like to buy a Porsche? It's almost new. There are only about eight hundred miles on it."

Richard didn't say anything, but he did get an "I'm sorry for your loss" look on his face and gave her a little shake of his head. Still wanting to draw him out, Freddie added that she was lucky that she had found two girls to move in with her. For some reason, she had overcome all remorse when it came to lying to Richard and so went on. "I put an ad in the paper last week. That house is so big and so expensive, but since it does have four bedrooms, I decided to take in boarders. Now that I got fired, I guess I can offer prepared meals too and maybe get an extra fifty a week from them. They're really nice girls. From New Jersey." Freddie put on a sort of "wounded, but I'll make it" smile and flashed it at Richard.

Richard gave a little start, which was very obviously fake, and picked his cell from his jacket pocket. Pretending to look at a text, he exclaimed, "Oh no." He shook his head and added. "Um. Listen. I really need to run. There has been a slight emergency with one of my clients. I'm so sorry. I'll call the agency! Bye."

Richard was gone. Freddie thought about the job he had claimed to have and wondered what an "information emergency" looked like.

She didn't think she would ever see him again, but did make a note with her recorder to let Angelique know he was off her list and that he was not to be trusted. Freddie knew he wasn't dangerous in the classical sense, just as a companion.

Freddie decided not to let the night go to waste and that she was going to get hammered. Before she started, though, she called over the bartender. Safety first, she told herself. Brea needed her now more than ever. "Hi." She read his name tag. "Brian." He smiled, in a silent hello. "Are you here till closing?"

"Yes, ma'am. Two AM."

"Good," she said. "Here's two hundred dollars. Keep pouring me tequila's until eleven o'clock or until I pass out. If I haven't passed out, bring me cold water and hot tea after that. In either case, at midnight, get me a cab. Keep whatever is left over. Oh, and I don't want to be bothered by any hormone-crazed land sharks."

"Yes, ma'am." Brian had seen this before. After all, it was a Dania Beach Chili's. There was more drama in this place than anywhere else on the entire east coast.

20

Thursday

Thursday morning came and went while Freddie slept. When she did get up, she found a note from Brea in which she explained that she had gotten herself up and gone to school with her friend Sarah. Freddie smiled the smile of a mother who had instilled self-reliance in her child. In addition, she admired Brea for being able to tell that this was a good day to exercise it.

After two strong cups of coffee and a lot of scratching at a pad of paper with her pencil, Freddie dialed a friend of hers who was a divorce lawyer. The conversation was a bit of a blur, but Freddie remembers saying, "Settle anything you want any way you want. All I need is full custody of Brea."

21

Bob, Again

By the time Saturday rolled around and it was time for Bob's third date, Freddie had descended into a blue funk. She could feel the drive to complete her project fading and was not looking forward to seeing Bob or anyone else again. Angelique had called Thursday with three new guys that she had scheduled for Sunday, Monday, and Wednesday. Freddie accepted the dates, but without the excited anticipation she had always felt before when she was going to meet someone new.

Freddie's third date with Bob started off to be a double-deck disaster. Fortunately, it ended better than either had expected. Bob had agreed to go on the date two weeks earlier, and he was the kind of guy that usually kept his promises. In the meantime, though, he had realized that Freddie was way out of his league. He would never have her as a girlfriend, and he would never get past one button on her blouse. Freddie was in the same frame of mind. Both of them were just going through the motions. Still, she turned on her recorder hoping that she could pull herself out of it and somehow complete her project. Bob had only one hope left. Somewhere after the third beer, he came out with it. They had been drinking beer because Freddie insisted that Bob needed more training before trying anything more dangerous again. She had told him that half-jokingly, but he readily agreed.

"Freddie." Bob mustered all his manhood. "You are one very attractive—no, exceptionally attractive—woman. On top of that,

103

you are pleasant to talk with, funny, smart, and most of all, you are forgiving." Bob hadn't been that straightforward with a woman in his life. "I know that I'm not the man for you. Hell, I'm not sure I'm anyone's man. But I think you probably have gotten to know me better than any woman since my mother." Freddie wondered where the heck this was going, but she was so gloomy herself, on the inside, that she found she really didn't care that much. Of course she didn't let that show and looked at Bob with intense, but fake, interest. "So, Freddie, what I am going to ask is really pretty dumb. But it's my last shot." He paused. "Do you have a sister? Maybe an ugly one? A cousin?" Bob pleaded with Freddie for help.

Freddie quipped back, "Well, since you're out, do you have a brother? Maybe taller? A friend who's a rugby player?"

After that exchange, they both laughed, and they both relaxed. The pretense of being on an arranged date had been broken. Both of them knew that they were not right for each other, and both of them knew that there was still a basis for perhaps a friendship. Freddie knew that she could transform Bob into a man who was at least socially competent. Now that she had made her decision about Noah and was going to be free soon, she also suspected that Bob would probably have more suitable friends than the ones she had been getting from the agency. The rest of the night was spent crying in their beer, sharing stories of Freddie's conquests and Bob's defeats. Freddie had tapped her microphone twice as a signal to herself that the game was over and what followed was genuinely personal. It would not be included in the project. She and Bob did, however, trade personal phone numbers with the intent of getting together once in a while and especially if either of them turned up a lonely cousin.

The next week was dismal for Freddie. She forced herself to go on the three dates Angelique had arranged. By the end of her last date on Wednesday, she had settled into a very low-key existence focused on completing the project with very little interest in actually enjoying it as she had done previously. Noah being gone was a mixed blessing. It gave her lots of time to think and lots of time to spend with Brea. It also gave her a strong feeling of insecurity. She decided that on Monday morning, after she dropped Brea off, she would start job hunting. Her resume was not strong, having held the job title of receptionist for fifteen years. She knew that her former employer was certainly not going to give her a positive recommendation. Freddie was determined, though, that she would not waste her energy any more on a nonproductive job.

22

Noah's Deal

By Friday afternoon, it felt as though her ship had righted itself. While her progress was sluggish, she was not dead in the water. She was still moving forward. She would survive. She had found her resolve and was rallying. That was when she got the call from her lawyer. "Hi, Freddie. It's Jennifer. I have news." Jennifer paused and Freddie's heart stopped. Jennifer went on, "I will let you decide if it is good news or not."

"Okay. Let me hear it," Freddie responded.

"Noah has accepted your demand for custody. He accepted your full custody with no restrictions. He expects that you will be practical about visits. He has also decided that you can stay in the house as long as you want or until Brea turns eighteen, and you can live there without paying rent. He will pay the utilities and all the maintenance. You can keep the Porsche and the Prius. If Brea goes to college, the arrangement will be extended until she graduates."

"Well, I would say that is good news so far. What else?" Freddie asked cautiously.

"There will be no alimony and no child support other than the house, utilities, and maintenance. Noah doesn't want to pay for college either. He gets full ownership of the company and retains title to the house and all of your nonpersonal belongings. After Brea turns eighteen or graduates, you are on your own."

It took only a minute to grasp the full meaning of Jennifer's message. It seemed like a very long minute. Freddie would need to provide little more than clothing and food for the next eight years or so. This was a good deal, she thought, and she said so. "Go ahead and draw it up, please." Jennifer advised her that a divorce in which nothing was being disputed would be final in about three weeks. She would not even need to attend the hearing.

Not thirty minutes later, she and Brea sat at the dining room table doing her math homework together when the phone rang again. It was Angelique. "Hello," Freddie forced herself to answer.

"Hey, Freddie. I think I forgot to tell you, but RJ sent me an e-mail a couple days after your first date. I'm sorry, but it ended up in my spam filter. Anyway, he had to go out on the ship for some research or something and was going to be at sea for a while. He said he had a great time and wanted to get together again when he got back. Did I tell you that?"

Freddie had thought she would not hear from RJ again. Now she was learning that he had tried to let her know that he enjoyed her company. She also realized that he had not received a reply for a couple weeks, and he was probably feeling exactly what she had felt up until thirty seconds ago. He probably felt he would not see her again. Freddie's emotions were in turmoil, but she didn't become angry with Angelique for her oversight. Instead, her subconscious came to her rescue, and her thoughts that her situation made her feel quite as though she was in a Shakesperian play made her smile. Calmly, but with a great deal of stifled anticipation, she said, "No, Angelique, you did not tell me that. What have you told RJ?"

"Actually, I haven't told him anything except that I would arrange another date. His ship is supposed to dock tonight and… let's see. Oh yeah. I did tell him I would ask if you were available this Saturday."

"Tomorrow?" Freddie said.

"Yeah. Tomorrow. Should I try and call him?"

Without even thinking about it, Freddie blurted out a perhaps overenthusiastic "Yes!"

"I'll call you back with a time and place," Angelique said and hung up.

"Good news, Mom?" Brea asked.

"Probably. We'll see," Freddie replied with a warm smile. "Now let's get back to your homework."

"Okay," Brea said but remained looking at her mom.

"What?" Freddie asked.

"It's nice to see you smile," Brea said. "It seems like it's been a while. That's all."

Freddie gave Brea a long hug and said, "Math. Now."

23

ORV Deepview

RJ's research cruise had gone pretty well. He actually liked being at sea. It was peaceful most of the time. Even when there was a storm, it was oddly peaceful for him. Sure, the ship rocked and pounded, but it was still just raw nature. He didn't find it threatening at all, perhaps because he found it entrancing instead.

As he watched the whitecaps break from the tops of the waves, he was reminded of his childhood. He had been a fearful youngster. Everything from spiders to riding a bicycle seemed to scare him. He had come to grips with it one day when his father was showing him how to sharpen a pocketknife. Of course he was afraid of the knife, but once he learned how to hold it and how to protect his hand with an old T-shirt, he realized that the fear came from the unknown, not from the threat itself. He found that knowledge was the key to courage. Later on, when he was told not to run with scissors in his hands, he calmly devised a way to do so safely. Watching the storm, he wondered if America would ever have put a man on the moon if fathers had not taught their sons to sharpen pocketknives.

RJ had been working on sound and light travel in something called the nepheloid layer. This is that special place between the normally clear ocean water and the muddy bottom. Crabs, shrimp, fish, and currents will often keep a little more material in the water right above the bottom than in waters higher up. RJ was trying to figure out if he could track submarines by using disturbances in the nepheloid layer that could last for weeks or months after a submarine had passed. Of course, he could not tell that to anyone.

On this trip, he had set up sensors vertically in the water column, which would be able to track disturbances in the water. Then, by sailing the research vessel over the top of the string of sensors, he could determine how far down the thing that nonscience majors called prop wash would go. Using some pretty simple math, he could then calculate how far down the prop wash from different configurations of submarine propellers would carry and whether or not it would disturb the nepheloid layer.

His research had actually started innocently enough when he was working with a colleague trying to determine how close an outboard motor propeller had to be to seagrasses before it would create enough force to dig it up, making a scar in the grassbed. Marine ecologists had learned that these submerged grasses can be severely damaged by too much scarring, and sometimes they can be eliminated entirely. RJ had been able to calculate that the propeller did not actually need to dig into the bottom. If the sediment was soft enough and the propeller was turning at the right speed, the prop wash alone would create the scar. RJ had helped out his colleague and then had taken his calculations to the Navy.

As the ship reentered the cell phone range of the coast, he powered up his antique flip phone. It was a much better design for use at sea because it was small, and the flip top protected the screen from shipboard hazards. It started beeping with message and voicemail alerts as soon as it found a tower.

RJ scanned down the list, looking for a particular call. He skipped past the one from the dean of the department with the red exclamation point and the one from his mother in Paducah.

Selecting the one labeled "Angelique" he pressed "listen." The past several days he had been wondering about whether or not he was going to be able to see Freddie again. He had received an e-mail from the agency, but then nothing further. He couldn't help but wonder if Freddie had crossed him off her list. He would have understood that because she was a very attractive woman and probably had lots of guys chasing after her. On the other hand, their first meeting was just exactly what he had been looking for in a relationship. She was comfortable.

Angelique's voice came on the line. "Hi, RJ. I think Freddie likes you." The lilt in her voice was just so high school it made RJ want to shut it off, but he let the message play. "Call me when you get back. We have saved Saturday night for you."

He was still three miles at sea, but within cell range, so he dialed her number. "Hello, this is Angelique. Please leave a message."

"RJ Hunter here. I just got into cell range and got your message. I'm still three miles out to sea and won't be at the dock for a while. Once we arrive, I need to offload. Please go ahead and let Freddie know that I am available and that I will be at the Marker One bar down by the channel at 6:00 PM tomorrow." RJ looked at his watch when he hung up. It was already after five, and he wasn't sure if Angelique would get the message to Freddie before tomorrow evening. He didn't yet know that Angelique worked more weekends than not. It was in the nature of the work. Within ten minutes, Angelique had texted Freddie, received a confirmation, and sent it back to RJ. RJ would not see the confirmation until morning. He had dumped his cell into its watertight dry bag and had begun the very hard and wet work of dismantling and packaging his equipment. Every piece of equipment that had been in the water was disassembled, cleaned, rinsed with freshwater, dried by hand, and packed into foam-filled crates. The team waited until they were near land to clean the gear because the cleaning process would use up almost all the freshwater on the ship. The captain would need to replenish the tanks, but having them near empty also gave him a chance to clean and disinfect them.

Freddie got a confirmation text from Angelique on Friday evening and immediately arranged for a sitter. Sarah's mom, Pauline, was busy so she had to call one of the local teenagers. Pauline had been very supportive ever since she realized that Noah had moved out. She was a big help with the logistics of single motherhood that had been thrust on Freddie. Noah was completely nonparticipatory. There was always a reason why he couldn't pick Brea up from school. In fact, Brea had not spent any time with her dad since he had moved out. The lie about him going on a business trip had worn itself out after the first week, and Freddie had come clean about their situation. Brea was trying to be strong about it, but it was still hard.

24

Marker One

RJ ran through the rest of his e-mails, voice mails, and texts early Saturday morning. He had worked late, but for some reason, he always woke up at 5:00 am no matter what time he went to bed. Coffee and a long game of catch-up was standard procedure after three weeks at sea. Sure, he knew he could get e-mails at sea. He could probably even forward his phone messages to his laptop while he was out, but the fact is that he didn't want to. He enjoyed what little isolation his cruises offered. RJ smiled when he came across the confirmation from Angelique. He was looking forward to seeing Freddie again.

RJ had been on the losing end of a string of bad experiences with women. He liked to think that he was capable of learning from his mistakes. He was amazed at how bad his luck had been and had finally decided to rely on his intellect more than luck and emotion. After a great deal of reflection on his errors in the selection of partners in the past, he realized he had missed one very important point: He needed to learn about what motivated a woman before he became too involved. He resolved not to overlook it in the future. He smiled as he recalled some old commercial from television, "The future is now." *Well*, he thought, *maybe it is and maybe it isn't.*

Julie, the sitter, arrived late Saturday afternoon right on time. Freddie kissed Brea good night and headed for the Porsche. She had once again put a lot of thought into her attire. Like most women, what they wore could change their whole attitude. She had learned this a long time ago and had used it to her advantage on numerous occasions. It took a little longer for her to figure out that her attire would also have an effect on the attitude of the people around her, especially if those people included single gentlemen.

Marker One was a small bar and restaurant associated with the marina. Not exactly a yacht club, but in Dania, almost every marina thought it was a yacht club. One thing that made it a special place was that the outside seating was on a wooden deck adjacent to the boat basin. Freddie chose casual: a loose and very lightweight blouse, tight white shorts, and sandals. All she needed to add was some windblown hair and big sunglasses, and she looked like a refugee from a resort club photo shoot.

RJ arrived at almost exactly the same time, and they went in together. Freddie thought to herself that he had obviously not become as enslaved to fashion as she had. He was in tennis shoes, jeans, and a T-shirt with the logo of a local dive shop on it. He was casual. He was comfortable. She liked it. She liked him, she admitted to herself.

He liked her too. He wasn't letting on too soon, but she could tell by the occasional glance, when she caught him at it, that he thought she was pretty hot. She also knew that he liked her for her and not just because she was pretty, but she couldn't tell why she knew that. Maybe it was for the same reason that she liked him for him instead of the muscles that were evident under his T-shirt. She thought he was both handsome and healthy, but the attraction came from somewhere else. They got a couple beers and headed out to the wooden deck that was suspended over the shoreline of the channel.

"It's good to see you again," RJ opened. "I hadn't heard anything for a couple weeks while I was out on cruise and didn't think you would call."

"That's funny because I thought the same thing. Angelique didn't tell me about your e-mail until just a couple days ago." Freddie paused and told RJ very sincerely. "I'm so sorry for the mixup."

"That's okay. It got straightened out, didn't it?" RJ said.

Freddie nodded with a smile. "So tell me about your cruise. What exactly do you do out there?" Freddie knew that the best way to get to know a man was to ask him a question and let him run with it. What she didn't know was that RJ knew that the rule held true for women too. Still, he took his turn and explained about the physics of light and sound and how chemistry, temperature, and movement can change the patterns. He left off the part about the secret submarine research. After all, he thought to himself in self-amusement, she might be a spy. He gave a pretty generic overview of the cruise and the research and then went into detail for one story. "One night, we decided to do a little sound transmissivity test. We hadn't planned on this test at all, and when the idea came up, it was already getting dark."

"Wait, wait, wait." Freddie said. "Refresh me on '*transmissivity.*'"

"Sorry." RJ grinned. "Sound is transmitted by a wave in the air that you can't see. These are not 'airwaves' like we hear about for radios, and they are not like waves in the ocean either. Sound is a compression wave. The wave doesn't go up and down like water, but the molecules move closer and farther apart to transmit the wave. It's like that set of steel balls on strings that executives play with. One ball hits the end of the row and the energy goes through the other balls, making the one on the other end jump. Get it?"

Freddie said. "Yeah. I remember now. And the more closely packed the molecules, the better the sound? Right?"

RJ smiled. "Not quite better. Pianists qualify sound as better. Physicists just accept it for what it is. Closely packed molecules make the sound travel faster. So a marble table will transmit sound faster than the air around it. A more pure substance, like the steel in a tuning fork, will make the sound more pure."

Freddie asked. "You mean that the tuning fork will give a sound that has only one frequency, right?"

RJ grinned. "Now you've got it. The end result is that sound travels faster in solids than in liquids. In gases, it is slowest and in a vacuum there is no sound at all. Transmissivity is the term we use to refer to these changes in the transmission of sound in different materials." He paused and asked, "Are you sure you want to get into this? I wouldn't suspect that this would be normal conversation for a date."

Freddie assured him. "While I appreciate the remedial short course, I do have a few college classes in the sciences, so I'm not lost yet. Please do go on. I find it fascinating."

"Okay. But stop me if it gets either boring or too technical." RJ was now teasing her. She knew it and used a rolling motion with her finger signaling him to continue.

"The next day, we had a full schedule, so instead of playing cards, which is what we usually did, we collected our hand held sound meters and put on our SCUBA gear. It's already sunset so we take lights too. So we jump in and then two of the guys set out a fishing net in the water. It was a seine with floats on top so it made something like a vertical wall made of netting. On one side, we had divers with an emitter, and on the other, we had divers with an array of receivers. Of course, all this had taken time and now the sun is fully set. We are doing this with underwater lights and with a little help from a full moon. It was actually sort of eerie."

RJ stopped to let the situation he described be fully appreciated and to get another beer. "You ready?" he asked.

Freddie grinned. "I was born ready."

RJ motioned to the waitress that they had run dry and then continued as she went to replenish their drinks. "So the emitters send out a pulse of sound. Now, sound is a wave, so when it hits something solid or semisolid, it can bounce back or it can bend. Almost every high school kid knows that. It can also be transmitted through the object—like hearing someone through a door or a window. What is less commonly known is that when the sound waves bend around things or are transmitted through things, the shape of the wave changes and just like two ocean waves in a storm that crash into each other, they can cancel each other out or at least change the height, or the amplitude, and the speed, or velocity, of the wave. In other words, it changes shape. Since this is sound, the shape of the wave is what generates what we call the pitch and intensity."

He paused again as the waitress brought the beer and looked at Freddie for confirmation that she was still interested. She was. He could tell by her eyes. "Our thought was this. What would happen to the sound wave when it went through the net? Each strand of netting would change small parts of the sound wave. We know that from basic physics. We also knew that if the diameter of the little strings in the net and the size of the mesh of the net was changed from one experiment to the next, it might change how much a sound wave was changed as it passed through it. Since there was only so much math you can do on a napkin in a wardroom, we decided to put it to the test. Our emitter pulsed a 'pure' sound wave, and our divers on the other side captured the result as a sound file."

"Wow," Freddie said. "That is really something else." She was genuinely and doubly impressed. First, she was impressed with RJ's imagination that led to his test and second that she was able to follow his explanation so easily. "So what was the answer? Did the sound change?"

RJ laughed a bit and said. "I have no idea. After we got out, we were tired, so we put up our gear and hit the sack. In the morning, we had to conduct our regularly scheduled experiment and so the sound files just had to wait. We'll have a grad student take a look at them next week."

"So you have a little science in that head of yours?" RJ switched the conversation to Freddie. It was her turn. "Tell me about it. Angelique said you work as a receptionist. Not many receptionists know a lot about physics. Some do, I suppose, but..." He realized he was starting to babble and shut up with a smile and a nod to Freddie.

"Well. Actually, I'm in college now." True statement, Freddie assured herself. "My interest is in literature." Also true, she assured herself again. She did not want to lie to RJ, but she couldn't just come completely clean about everything. There was too much at stake. RJ was turning out to be a little different than her other dates. His part in her project was becoming more significant, and she couldn't jeopardize all her work on a whim. "I've completed all my classes." True. "All I need to do is to write a term paper."

Almost true, she consoled herself. "It's really complicated and pretty long. I think of it as my book that no one will ever read."

"I'd love to read it," RJ said without hesitation.

Freddie gave him her best "think about something else" smile with a wink and said, "Maybe when it's done."

RJ could tell that she was not interested in opening up yet. Her short answers and changing the subject gave her away. He could also tell she was interested in him. That impression was solidified by her next question. "I need to ask you something. You're a good-looking guy. You're smart. You have a sense of humor, a good job, and quite frankly, you are quite comfortable to be with, so why do you need the services of Angelique?"

RJ thought to himself, *Good. If she is comfortable enough with me to ask a question like that, our relationship just might work out.* A thousand thoughts can go through a mind in a nanosecond, and this was happening now to RJ. He played with his beer a bit and looked into her eyes. She was what his grad students called a "stone-cold fox." Tonight, she was certainly not dressed fancy, and she had little to no makeup. Those white shorts of hers, though, had caught his attention. He often wondered why women would wear something that would put certain body parts on display for all the world to see, and then get upset when a man stared at them a bit too long. RJ's hormones and his intellect were in an all-out war with each other. What snapped him out of it was the recollection that this was a war he had lost before. "I'm looking for a friend," he said. *True,* he assured himself.

RJ could tell from the inquisitive look on Freddie's face that this was not going to be enough of an answer, so he continued. "I'm the kind of guy who has lots and lots of acquaintances and only a few closely held friends. Yes, it is true that my job is a good one, and I meet a lot of people there. Most of them are graduate students in their early to mid-twenties. The faculty is mostly married or…" He stopped himself, his mind racing again.

He had always been bothered by the self-importance that so many faculty members had adopted once they earned their doctorate degrees. It was one thing to be smart and dedicated enough to do the work to get the degree and that was to be respected. It was another to demand that everyone in the building call you "doctor" just because you went to college longer than they had. Some of these guys even made the junior professors call them "doctor" or "professor." It reminded him of when he was in the Navy. Some of the officers made it their sworn duty to know the lineal number of every other officer on the base or ship. It was the lineal number, or the number assigned to match the order of who got promoted first, that determined that one officer was superior to another officer when they both held the same rank. The one with the lower lineal number had been promoted first, so he was in charge. RJ had decided a long time ago that that sort of behavior was just too much like a bunch of second graders establishing pecking order based on which one was taller. Not wanting to be openly derisive of his colleagues, he changed the end of his sentence from "snooty," which was the word he almost said. Instead he concluded with "Really busy with their work."

"When we do go out for a beer or have a faculty gathering, all we seem to talk about is our research. I was hoping to find a friend who would like to talk about other things and do other things. I am looking for someone to go to museums with and go to the park with or to a movie. A guy in my position just doesn't meet people that fit that description."

"So hang on there, dude," Freddie said with a playful grin. "Are you telling me you paid all that money to the service and you're not even looking for a girlfriend?"

RJ's laughter was quick to start, but he let it tail out a bit because those shorts and her long legs were taking their toll on his resolve. "Not exactly. Let me clarify. Yes, I would like to have a woman in my life. For the exact same reasons that I can't find a friend within my existing circles, I will never be able to find a girlfriend. I need to expand my circles before finding either one. I need to put myself in a position of meeting people who are not scientists, not physicists, not faculty, and who are not in their twenties. I need to meet people in a different way than trolling the bars. The agency seemed like it would cast the widest net. All the normal social barriers are gone, and Angelique just puts people together to see what happens. Looking for a friend first seemed like the way to go. I would like more real friends, and if one of them happens to also become a girlfriend, or to introduce me to a girl who fits that role, then so be it. If nothing else happens, I get to meet a lot of new people with different interests, and I get to make friends with the ones who aren't simply out trolling for men. Those women are pretty easy to spot, and then I don't call Angelique back. I didn't get that feeling from you, though. You're easy to talk with and easy to be with."

RJ stopped, and they looked at each other for a long time. Finally, RJ added, "Now it's your turn. You are a beautiful woman. You are congenial, conversational, and intelligent. What on earth are you doing using the agency? You could get all the men you want just walking down the street."

Freddie thought this might come up. She had no delusions about her attractiveness and had worked hard over the years to keep it from driving her to narcissism. Her own upbringing had made this easier because her parents had instilled in her a solid set of standards by which she measured conduct and self-importance. Still, she couldn't dodge the question. It was a fair question. He had just laid his intentions on the table quite honestly and deserved the same from her. She hated to do it, but she still couldn't show all her cards. She realized that she was even going to need to lie about the status of her divorce, but justified it with the knowledge that the divorce was not reversible. It was going to happen.

"My story is almost the same story as yours, RJ. I'm a divorced single mom who used to work with my ex-husband. All the people I know are either his friends or are people I met at the office. The other parents at Brea's school, that's my daughter, Brea, are married, and the ones that aren't are usually other moms like me. The truth is that there aren't many single dads out there taking their kids to school. So, like you, I needed to broaden my circle. I do need to admit one thing."

Freddie gave RJ a big grin and continued. "You are right. I could get laid any time I want. I suppose I am fortunate because I have kept myself in good shape and have been blessed with a nice face and good hair, but it is also a bit of a curse. I spent too many years with a husband who never appreciated my mind. I don't want to make the same mistake with someone I might find in a bar."

The rest of the evening was not quite so intense, but it was revealing. As it progressed, both RJ and Freddie got to know each other a little better. RJ told stories of being on the farm. He related his escapades, like skinny-dipping with his sister's best friend down in the swimming hole and making a bobsled run that started on the roof of the barn and ended in the pasture. She told stories about her childhood in Indiana. She did have to confess, though, that even she wasn't really sure what a Hoosier was. Freddie talked about Brea with abandon, and RJ could tell that her girl was the focal point of her life.

He talked about how he worked his way through college waiting tables, tending bar, and working in landscaping. She told him about how she had worked her way through college as a transcriptionist at the local doctor's office. She had also taken in piece work and had typed a lot of depositions for a local attorney. She skirted her relationship with Noah and only talked about the business in general terms, never mentioning either of them by name. While she never said as much, she allowed RJ to have the impression that she had not finished college, dropping out to get married. She let him think that she was now simply finishing her undergraduate degree.

Later that night, at home, after putting Brea to bed, she sat in her study downloading her recording of the evening. She could feel the tears welling up in her eyes. RJ was being as open and honest as anyone she had ever met. He as much as admitted that he wanted her in the typical male way, but he had set himself on a mission of finding a friend. He wanted someone he could share his nonscience moments with and to not feel pressured by the requirements of the mating dance. That must come first. In repayment for his honesty and openness, she had given him only as much truth as she could without exposing her project.

25

Sunday

Sunday morning, Angelique got text messages from both Freddie and RJ. She smiled the contented smile of a successful matchmaker and thought that perhaps she had put two people together who might actually have a future. Her job was rewarding, but it also was filled with so many failures. She retyped RJ's suggestion into the message to Freddie. It read: "Next Saturday. 9:00 am. Boca Vista Nature Park. OK to bring Brea."

Freddie responded almost immediately: "OK. No Brea this time. Maybe next time."

Angelique passed the information on to RJ. It was almost time for her to step aside and let these two make their own arrangements, she thought. The service made each client sign a contract not to share personal contact information until relationships started to develop in a positive manner. That was the agency's way of protecting clients and of reducing their own liability. She was just about to ask Freddie if she wanted to do that when a second text popped up. It was Freddie again. "Do I have any other dates this week? Next week?" Angelique rescinded her prior thought about direct contact and for the first time questioned Freddie's motivation. She had never been enigmatic in the past, but now she seemed to be stepping out of character. It was clear from her conversations and e-mails that Freddie liked RJ, so why would she be asking about other men? Angelique told herself that it was not her concern and went about setting Freddie up for Monday, Wednesday, and Friday. By noon, Freddie had accepted all three dates.

Freddie looked at the screen on her computer that displayed her calendar. By the end of the week, she would only have seven more dates to go on, and she could start to wrap things up. By the end of the week, Freddie had completed the three dates with her new guys and had also filed twelve job applications. She had drawn a line in her own personal sand with her job hunt. She was not going to accept another temp job or secretarial/receptionist position. She filled out her applications with the notation that she had a BA and expected an MS within four months. But she was having a heck of a time with her resume. It still said "Receptionist: 15 years." There was still an annotation that the potential employer should not ask her former employer for a reference.

The week passed slowly. In fact, Freddie realized, it was agonizingly slow. Still, she consoled herself; it had passed without any major derailments to her plans.

26

A Walk in the Woods

Saturday morning came, and Freddie dropped off Brea at Pauline's to play with Sarah. She promised to be back right after lunch. The drive out to the nature park in her Porsche was relaxing and exciting at the same time. She loved the way the car handled and the feeling of freedom that a convertible could give. She also liked the school-girl feeling of anticipation that she had been unable to subdue.

RJ was sitting at a picnic table when Freddie drove up. He was feeding a squirrel, which he had apparently coaxed right up on top of the table. When Freddie arrived, the squirrel took off, then looked back, wondering if she had food too. "Good morning," they said in unison.

"You look nice," he said.

"Thanks." She smiled back at him, and off they went into the park. They walked for almost a quarter mile in silence, just enjoying the woods, the quiet, and the scenery.

"I didn't expect a physicist to be a nature buff," Freddie said. "It's nice."

"Freddie, let me ask you. What is physics if it is not nature? Nature is a great deal more than just plants and animals, isn't it?"

She wanted to take his hand as they walked but resisted. He wanted to explore friendship first, and she needed to finish her project. "I suppose it is," she replied. "I never really thought about it like that."

"Oh sure," he added. "Look at the soil here. Gravity, of course, holds it on the earth, but friction holds it together. When the sun comes through the canopy and hits it, the photons warm the soil so seeds can sprout. The heat creates evaporation putting water vapor into the air. If the air had no water in it, the humidity would drop so low that both plants and animals would dehydrate and possibly die. Those same photons are captured in the leaves, which give the plants the energy to grow. When a seed falls on the soil and then a light rain falls, the rain buries the seed by microerosional forces. It's all force and matter and the stuff of physics. Look at that bird. It uses physics to sit on that branch, but it is a physics born of practicality, not ingenuity. Well, unless you subscribe to one of the God theories of creation."

"What do you mean?" Freddie inquired.

"Look at how he sits on that branch. Have you ever wondered if his little feet get tired from being clenched all day?" She nodded and he continued, "You see a bird's feet are built with tendons, muscles, and bones just like ours are, but with one big difference." Freddie's eyes were wide with wonder and anticipation. RJ went on. "Tendons are like big rubber bands. They just stretch and snap back to where they want to be. Muscles, on the other hand take energy to contract. If you completely relax your own hand"— he reached down and took her hand, laying it flat, palm up and cradled in the palm of his own hand—"you see that your fingers are partially curled." Freddie glanced down at her hand. It looked small cradled in his strong fingers. Her gaze was drawn back to RJ's face as he went on. "That's because when the muscles relax, the tendons pull the fingers into that position. It takes no energy at all to stay that way. Well, in the foot of that bird, the tendons are built so that they completely close his claw when the muscles are relaxed. A bird on a branch is not squeezing the branch any more than my hand is squeezing yours."

Freddie retrieved her hand and gave RJ a crooked grin. "That's actually quite fascinating, but I was asking what you meant with your comment about God theory."

"Oh. That." He pulled an orange from his pocket and played with it a bit as he started to explain. "It's simple. Of all the theories of how we are here there is only one thing that can separate them into two main groups." RJ stopped and pointedly said to Freddie. "Oh, yes, make sure you catch that I said 'how' we are here and not 'why' we are here."

She nodded and he continued, "These two groups are the God and no-God theories of creation. In the God cluster, there is an almighty being which creates everything from scratch. Even in polytheistic societies like the ancient Greeks, Romans, and Egyptians, there was always one of the gods that was more powerful than the others. In the no-God cluster, the existence of the universe is attributed to big bangs; cosmic explosions; supernovas; planetary formation; and the semirandom results of physics and chemistry giving rise to biochemistry, life, and evolution. In the no-God belief system, there are no souls, or spirits, and there is no spirit world. They cannot be seen, and so the theory is that they are not there."

"Well, that sounds simple enough," Freddie said as she poked him in the ribs to emphasize her point. "You must be in the no-God group being a scientist and a physicist. I'm sort of a reformed Catholic myself. I was raised Catholic, but I've recovered."

RJ laughed at her statement but went on to correct her assumption. "Actually, no. My beliefs are in the God group. You see the logic in the no-God group has some real fatal flaws that no self-respecting scientist should be able to accept." RJ started peeling the orange. "Want some?"

"No, thanks," Freddie replied, "but I do want to hear more about this God, no-God logic."

"Well, it's simple actually. In the God group, I fall into the category of a man who believes God made the universe but not in seven days. That puts me at odds with some other members of the God group and specifically those who reject evolution. I fully accept evolution, but I think of it less as the survival of the fittest and more like the elimination of the weakest. In environments that are biologically forgiving, like warm seas with lots of food, there are many different kinds of animals. This isn't because the fittest survive. It's because there are no forces eliminating the less fit species. Everyone survives. In the Arctic, there are fewer species because the unfit are eliminated. But I digress."

"Really?" Freddie thought to herself, but it was still interesting to listen to him talk.

"My first logical task then is to reconcile evolution and creation. This is quite easily done using the Bible itself as my source book. The Bible is said to be inspired by God, Himself. Any good Catholic, Christian, Jew, or Muslim will tell you that. I ask simply if it was inspired or dictated? I grant that the Ten Commandments may have been given under dictation, but the rest is probably more on the inspired side. Now we ask who wrote these inspired words. We don't need a name. All we need to know is that this person, whoever he was, lived at a time when mankind, such as it was, didn't even have words to represent a number greater than a thousand. No one understood or could even conceive of a planetary system, much less a universe. The prevailing theory was that the stars were holes in the firmament through which the light of God shone down on earth. So now, God, wanting to give his people a guide, has a problem. If he dictates the story of creation in real time, using physics and chemistry, not only will no one alive at the time be able to read it and understand it, but no one could write it either. The scientific vocabulary simply didn't exist. So, God...probably...I don't pretend to speak for God, I am just presenting my theory and logic, God decides to inspire man, or I should say, some men, to write about how He was able to bring forth life and mankind from nothing. The guy writing it down gets the gist of the story through the divine inspiration, but has to tell it in his own words in a way that will be accepted by the other people.

"Many people in the God group hold that an all-powerful being could easily have created the world in seven days. I agree. However, an all-powerful being who can conceive of and create a system of physical and chemical laws that would ultimately lead to a big bang, planetary formation, and evolution is rather more impressive. Since time means little to God, in that He needn't be in a hurry, and the human scribe cannot conceive of billions or trillions of years, the combined story of creation and evolution makes more sense." He looked at Freddie. She wore an expression that was a mixture of amazement and attempted comprehension. "At least it makes more sense to me," he added.

RJ saw a young butterfly in the path. It had apparently only recently metamorphosed and was not eager to fly. He quickly crushed a wedge of his orange between his first two fingers, popped the pulp in his mouth, and reached his hand down to the butterfly. She climbed onto his fingers dabbling at the orange juice with her proboscis. RJ held it close so that both he and Freddie could watch. After a few moments, he put her back down in the path and went on.

"On the no-God side, as you intimated, there are mostly scientists. Unfortunately, the logic of science has been abandoned in the establishment of the no-God theory by the very scientists who support it. Let me ask you a question. In the universe of scientific achievement, there is only one discipline that contains absolute proofs of its theories. Which one is that?"

Freddie was still somewhat stunned by the casual display of butterfly whispering but collected her thoughts, blurting out, "Mathematics! Everything else is just theory that seems to work pretty well."

"Correct, grasshopper." He grinned. "With that in mind, we ask how science makes progress. Simply put, people observe, create an hypothesis or story to explain the observation, and then test the story by doing experiments designed to destroy the story. If the story holds up, then it is deemed to be probably a good story but only because it explains the observation with either few or no contradictory flaws. Examining the history of mankind, we find hundreds of thousands of reports of experiences that are completely unexplainable by the laws of physics and chemistry. These can be ghost stories, miracles, mind reading, and even the weird relationship that twins have."

RJ looked at Freddie for confirmation that she was following his thought. "What they have in common is that they are stories about the spirit and the spirit world. Looking inside our own being, we recognize that there is an entity that is somehow separate from the physical constraint of our bodies. I don't question for a moment that many of these stories we hear might be completely fabricated, but are we to say that they all are? The laws of probability are against it. So our observation is that there is something going on. We have, over time, labeled it the spiritual world. The fact that we cannot see it or sense it is of no consequence. We cannot see gravity either. Just because our biological senses cannot sense this spirit world, its existence cannot be dismissed."

"Why not?" Freddie interjected.

RJ nodded. "Because doing so also dismisses each and every one of the independent observations. What must be taken into account is the observed probability that many people actually can sense certain aspects of this spiritual world. In short, the hypothesis that we have a spiritual sense that has yet to be defined by scientists working in the physical world is still a better story than the one that says it's all hokum. It's a better hypothesis because it accounts for the observations. I, as a scientist, am forced to reach this conclusion simply because, according to the rules of science, the observations are better explained by our inability, or failure, to understand and measure the spiritual side of nature than by a denial of the observations themselves. If we applied our inability to measure something as the acid test of its existence, we would not have developed even a rudimentary understanding of things like quantum physics or subatomic particles."

"Um, yeah. That's pretty much the way I had it figured out too. You just said it a lot better than I could." Freddie giggled and poked him in the ribs again. *I've got to stop that,* she said to herself. That's what high school girls do to the boys in the hall when they want to get their attention.

The rest of the hike was much less intellectually taxing. They talked about the Miami Heat a little, but Freddie learned that RJ really didn't care for basketball. He liked the football games, and the Marlins too, but had a hard time convincing himself to pay what amounted to $37 per gallon of beer while complaining about $3.70 a gallon for gasoline. All told, the gasoline was the better value. Freddie learned that RJ liked to be consistent in his logic. Unlike a lot of people, he let logic, and reason, guide him instead of using logic and reason to try and explain a bad decision. But then again, he didn't. Or maybe he did. It all got confused in her head.

Because RJ had accepted the probable existence of a spiritual world, he also was forced to accept the probability that each of us might be able to enhance our individual abilities in using or accessing that spiritual sense. He had subsequently spent many hours developing his own skills, which only served to add to his body of evidence. By the time she got around to asking him about how to do this, they had reached the end of the trail, and it was time to go.

She had to get Brea, and he had to go grade some papers. RJ never, ever let his graduate students do that. He took his responsibilities as a faculty member very seriously. As their professor, RJ felt personally responsible for the intellectual development of every one of his students, whether they were graduates or undergraduates. He promised her he would help her with discovering her spiritual sense on their next date but made a point of saying the next time we "hang out" together instead of referring to it as a date.

Almost as an afterthought, when Freddie mentioned picking up Brea, RJ said that he really thought she would have liked the hike in the woods, and it was too bad she couldn't come. Next week, though, there was an exhibit at the Miami Seaquarium that might be fun, and Freddie should ask her along. Freddie calculated that this was her third date with RJ, so her commitment to the project had been met and it wouldn't hurt to include Brea, so she agreed. They decided to trade phone numbers and promised not to tell Angelique.

Before RJ even got out of the parking lot, his phone rang. "Hello?"

"Hey, it's Freddie. I forgot something. I was going to ask you if you would do me a favor. I need help with my resume. I'll be graduating soon, and I want to have it look a little better than what I have now. Do you think you could take a look at it?"

"Sure, I would be happy to," RJ said. "How do you want to do this?"

"I'll meet you at the library around two thirty. Is that okay?"

"I'll be there," RJ said and hung up. He couldn't shake the feeling that Freddie was still not telling him everything there was to tell. Maybe he would get to know more by helping with the resume.

Freddie picked up Brea and took her home. It was Brea's time to do her weekend homework and so Freddie got her all situated at the dining room table before she headed into the study. Freddie cropped out the part in her resume that included her job history and put it in a separate document. This way, RJ would not see her education history. While doing this, she promised herself that she would tell him eventually.

Back in the kitchen, she told Brea that she had to run down to the library. She made sure Brea had her phone nearby in case she needed something and assured her she would be back inside an hour. During the past year or so, Freddie had taken to leaving Brea alone for short periods of time. Unknown to Brea and to the credit of Freddie's parenting skills, these had slowly become longer over the months, and now both Freddie and Brea were pretty comfortable with Brea being alone for up to two hours as long as Freddie was available by phone. Freddie kept reminding herself that Brea was still ten, but she also wanted to let her develop at her own pace and this felt right to both of them.

At the library, Freddie was almost effervescent in her thanks for his help. He was a bit let down, though, when he saw that all she had brought was her work history. She was still not ready to completely open up, he told himself. He put himself to the task at hand and let her decide when it was time to let him in.

"First of all," RJ instructed her, "leave off her part-time jobs in college."

Freddie looked dismayed. "If I do that, then the only job left is the receptionist job. That's kinda thin, don't you think?"

Nodding, RJ asked, "What did you actually do?"

RJ listened intently, taking a few notes, for five minutes as Freddie told him about her multiple roles. She was the lead employee in bookkeeping, scheduling, inventory control, and most importantly in marketing. RJ was a very good listener, and when Freddie finished, he rewrote her job description.

Job Title: None

Job Duties: The duties of my previous position were expansive and included tasks normally assigned to several more standard job categories. The primary responsibility of the position was to assure that all aspects of the corporation which did not occur on the engineering floor were accomplished in a timely manner. These tasks included the lesser ones of client hospitality and scheduling, financial record keeping and financial management, payroll, accounts receivable and payable, as well as product shipping and parts receiving. Scheduling of staff and production targets was a secondary function. The most important and rewarding of these tasks was that of preparing and launching effective advertising and marketing campaigns. The success of these campaigns is evident in the level of success achieved by the corporation.

When he finished, he asked her about whether or not she was going to put in there that she had written, or was writing, a book. Freddie said it would never be published, so what was the point? RJ let it go.

"Then we're done!" RJ said. "Do you like it?"

"I do!" Freddie beamed. "Of course, there is still the problem of getting a good reference from my old boss who is also my ex-husband."

"No worries," RJ stated as a simple matter of fact. "Under reason for leaving, write that you are bound by a confidentiality agreement. Then list professionals from some of the other corporations that you did business with as references. I would make sure to list the advertising, CPA, and shipping firms more so than other engineering and production firms."

Freddie thanked him graciously and said she would get back to him about the Seaquarium. RJ, ever the gentleman, thanked Freddie for the opportunity to help.

Back at home, Freddie realized that indeed it was time to begin actually writing her book. While Brea watched an afternoon movie, Freddie retired to her study. She still had a few dates to go, but she would be done by the end of next week. There was time available now, and she figured she could just go ahead and get started. For the next three days, Freddie organized her notes. Getting fired had turned into a blessing in disguise, even if she had not quite come to grips with the associated divorce. She now had plenty of time to get this done. She had twenty-five names, and with three dates this week and four more next week, she was done.

First, she took the names and put them into groups. Her first grouping was by age, then income, then marital status: single, divorced, widowed. She wouldn't need these statistics until later but thought it was a good idea to get the information collected into one place. Next she started to sort the men out by some intangible traits. Some were shy, some were aggressive. Some just wanted to get laid. No, she corrected herself. All of them wanted to get laid. They just all showed different levels of restraint. As soon as she came to this realization, one of the major conclusions of her project became clear. This whole experience was just like high school.

Finally, she started doing profiles. For this job, she needed to review the tapes of the dates and that would take an unbelievable amount of time. Twenty-five guys with three dates each, and each date being about three hours amounted to about two hundred and twenty-five hours of recordings.

Going to her study, she grabbed a stack of papers and a glass of bourbon before finding her place at her desk. Sipping the drink, she studied the pages before her intently. These were her notes on male behavior patterns taken from about eight different textbooks on the subject. Sometimes she wished they would agree with each other a bit more, but then if they did, she would not have a project to pursue and would probably always be a receptionist in her husband's business. Or, she corrected herself, in someone else's business.

She decided to start with profiling Richard. Richard was handsome, healthy, and in his mid-thirties. He had what her grandmother used to call the "gift of gab," meaning that he was a talker. His conversational skills were highly developed. He had obtained all the social graces of a person who was born to it. In his mannerisms, however, she noted that there were telltale speech patterns that led her to believe that he was in fact born into a less fortunate set of circumstances. For example, he pronounced the word "escape" as if it were spelled "exscape." This slang was common in some of the less well-educated social groups in the United States. He was quite obviously of Latino descent, genetically, and Freddie had guessed he probably was originally from Puerto Rico but may have lived in one of the larger northern cities for a while before coming to the Miami area. There were other minor speech patterns that supported this hypothesis, but in truth, where he was from was irrelevant to the project. In summation, Freddie concluded that Richard was the male version of a gold digger. He had put on airs of wealth and social prowess, selected women from the agency who had similar profiles to each other, and he intended to marry whatever wealth he could charm into doing so. Should he fail in his matrimonial goals, at least he got laid a lot. She was sure of that.

Richard had one skill: charm. If he had made different choices as a young man, he probably could have made a very good advertising executive. Instead, he had simply taken the easier choice of becoming a parasite on lonely women. Richard's profile ended with a note that he was the sole example of this type of person among those she had interviewed.

Jake's profile was much more brief. Jake was a predator. He had paid his way onto the rolls of the agency. He was looking for cheap, rough sex, and that was all. For the price of a few drinks and dinner, he expected and probably often got exactly what he was looking for. This conclusion was partially conjecture on Freddie's part. She was, however, well aware of the depth and completeness of the dating services questionnaires and interviews. Angelique was a professional, and she was probably very much aware of both Jake's and Richard's intentions. Why Angelique had matched her with Jake had not become clear at all until her date with Terry. Jake, like Richard, was the only example of the predator type. As she concluded his profile, she made a note to make sure the agency had her project files so that their screening process could be improved.

Terry was just like Jake, except that Terry ran a better game. Jake expected an after-dinner romp because of some primal idea that he was the man and if he paid for dinner, he got what he wanted. Terry took a little time and earned his time in the sack. He had no scruples about how he got there, but he was after the same thing. Freddie had not realized being paired with Jake and Terry had been simple economics. In Angelique's world, her boss signs a contract that includes a guarantee of three dates a month. In Terry's case, if there were no women in his age bracket available, Angelique was forced to at least offer him a date or he would get his entire fee refunded. In Jake's case, Angelique sort of knew he was a scumbag but figured Freddie was better equipped to handle him than were some of the other girls. Freddie got Jake because Angelique was nervous about giving him to someone more naïve. The profile Freddie wrote on Terry included a section on how an otherwise capable person could wind up in his sixties and still be fixated on casual sex with women he had just met. Terry's group contained three others, all of whom had a history of failed relationships in their past. The common thread was that the relationships had all failed because these men had placed a high priority on the sexual component of the relationship and had spent little time on learning about the actual person. Freddie was tempted to add Noah to this group but resisted. She figured he would end up there in the near future anyway.

Her profile of Harold was subtitled: Teacher or Politician. After reviewing her notes and listening to the tapes, she realized that Harold exhibited many of the same conversational traits that politicians exhibited when running for office. Ever since Freddie started taking her classes again, she had been paying a lot more attention to human interaction, especially in conversation. Over the course of that first year, she had had several conversations with Brea's teachers and had also had several conversations with the university faculty. During the summer, before the November elections, she also caught several of the debates and candidate forums that had been held. She smiled with the memory—it was just like RJ had said: observe, hypothesize, and test. In her observations, she had noted that neither teachers nor politicians ever actually answer a question as it is asked. The politician might offer a quick "sure" as a short answer, but then he would launch into something that always seemed to begin with "But let me tell you about…" and off he would go on his own agenda. The teacher would most often reword or restructure your question. These often started off with "I think what you're trying to ask is…" She often wanted to scream at Brea's teacher. "No! That's *not* what I'm trying to ask! I asked about what I want to know about, now just give me the answer!" But she didn't. She just smiled and said "thank you." Harold's version had been a little different. He had said more than once that "A better question would be…" after which he asked and answered his better question.

Freddie reflected for a moment as she finished Harold's profile. He and RJ did have some things in common. They both knew a lot of stuff about a lot of stuff. But that was about as far as it went. Harold shared his knowledge in a very remote way. He was in the same room, but he never actually had a conversation with Freddie. He had talked to his drink, to his fork, to his dinner, and even to his napkin but seldom looked directly at Freddie. He shared his knowledge on a one-way street. He talked and others listened. RJ, on the other hand seldom looked anywhere but directly into her eyes when they were conversing. It had been different, of course, on the nature walk because of needing to watch where they were going. In the restaurant, she had noticed that he was aware of everyone and everything in the room, but she also noticed that, even at this early stage of their friendship, his eyes came back to hers very regularly and repeatedly. As the evening had progressed, RJ's eyes spent more and more time on her than on the rest of the room.

Acknowledging to herself that her thoughts had strayed from her writing, she now wondered if RJ and Harold should be in the same group. There was one more of her dates who could either be in this group with Harold and RJ or be in Terry's group. He was a local politician. His mannerisms in conversation were like Harold's but his intentions were closer to Terry's. The most difficult element of Harold's profile was why he was using the dating service in the first place? Sure, he wanted to get laid. He had the same urges as everyone else. Finally she concluded that Harold was using the service as a last resort. She decided RJ would not be in this group because of his motives. Freddie put RJ's write-up aside.

Bob was the pathetic one. He and three other guys were in a group she subtitled: Needing therapy. Bob's self-esteem was almost nonexistent. In his head, he was fine, but when it came time to demonstrate self-confidence and to become engaged in a conversation or a relationship, he succumbed to a pressure to perform that effectively nullified his good traits. Freddie was happy that she and Bob had come to a point where they could be friends. She never had been able to determine where his pressure had come from in the first place. Maybe it came from his childhood or a series of bad experiences in high school. All she knew for certain was that it was there and that was sufficient for the project.

Freddie hit "Save all" and shut down the computer for the night.

RJ left the library feeling good about helping Freddie and feeling somewhat unsettled about the limited version of the resume. He was perfectly comfortable with Freddie, and it seemed that she was comfortable with him. For the life of him, he could not put his finger on what was holding her back. *What was it?* he asked himself time and again. *What was it that she was not willing to tell him?*

RJ came home from the office where he had graded student papers and went out on the back porch. He had a modest little place that fronted on an unofficial nature preserve. The developer who built the subdivision had been forced by the county to set aside this little piece of wooded wetland, and RJ, frankly, was glad for it. His view was trees and birds instead of the backyard of the next guy. Sure, there were mosquitoes, but "That's why God made DEET," he said to himself. RJ had his binoculars, his camera, a short glass of Panamanian rum, and thought that this was about as good as it gets. Still, it was moments like this and places like this that he wanted to share with a friend. His conversation with Freddie had really clarified some things in his mind, or he corrected himself, in his spirit. His friends were great. That wasn't the problem. He admitted to himself that he really was looking for that person with whom he could have that spiritual connection. They were few and, unfortunately, far between. He had felt it before. He knew it was there. Perhaps that's why he was able to reconcile the physical world and the spiritual world so easily. He wasn't relying on the observations of other people. He had his own.

He also knew that simply having that spiritual level of connectivity was not all that it took. He knew men with whom he felt that connection. But there were only two of them making them even more rare than the women. He also had felt the connection with women who had turned out to be completely unsuited for him; some were even what he would call evil. The connection itself was just the sensory component. He had often pondered if the feeling was being commonly mistaken for love and therefore contributing to the high divorce rate when the couple realized their mistake. There was also an emotional component. He had eventually been able to use the emotional part to determine what could only be called "goodness." He remembered reading a book once where this was called "seeing someone with the heart and not the eyes." It was this part that he felt strongly with Freddie. He not only saw her beauty with his eyes, but he sensed her beauty with his soul. It was there that the conflict arose. He sensed her goodness. That expressed itself with an overwhelming feeling of just being comfortable with her. He also sensed that she was troubled. Her troubles expressed themselves in him as his feeling that she was still keeping things from him.

His consolation was that he could not change these things and so his best course of action was to accept Freddie for who she was and wait to see if she would do the same.

27

Saturday at the Seaquarium

RJ drove up to Freddie's house out in Westin at 10:00 am on Saturday morning. Freddie came out and greeted him happily. "A Land Rover, I see. Nice wheels." RJ said it was an okay ride and started to tell her about it but was interrupted when Brea bounced out of the house and down the walk. "You must be Brea," he said.

"Yes, sir, I am," she said and stuck out her hand. "And you must be my mom's new friend."

"That's right. I'm Randy, but my friends call me RJ. What do you think you'll call me?"

"I'm not sure. We'll see." Brea quipped and went to the Land Rover. "Are we going?"

The three of them looked like a poster for the Seaquarium. All of them dressed in shorts, Hawaiian shirts, sunglasses, and sandals. They climbed into the Land Rover, and off they went. It was a long drive from Westin to the Seaquarium, and they spent the time singing along with the radio, which was tuned to the oldies station. In RJ's mind, the trip to the Seaquarium was a big step forward in Freddie's relationship with him. She was willing to let him meet Brea. The long trip meant that she was comfortable enough to commit to a situation that would be impossible to bail out on if it didn't go well. He suspected she had been hurt in the past and was just being careful. That was understandable since he was doing exactly the same thing.

The day went exceptionally well. Brea was inquisitive. RJ was full of answers. Freddie was mostly being observant. She was enjoying watching how well RJ and Brea were getting along.

At one point, Brea said, "RJ? How did you get so smart? I want to be smart."

RJ laughed. "I'm not particularly smart. I'm just very, very curious. I like to learn new things, and I don't care if I learn them from a book or from going out and exploring. I was very fortunate to learn that I loved reading when I was only a child. In fact, I was about your age. I decided right there and then that I wanted to learn as much about it as I could. So I did."

"But," she countered, "you know so much more than most of mom's friends. How do I get that smart?"

RJ stopped and knelt down on one knee beside her. "Listen, Brea. You are going to hear all kinds of talk about IQ points, AP classes, IB classes, and how one university is better than another. People will tell you that you can't get ahead if you don't attend the best high school and university and get the best tutors and all kinds of things. But here's the truth. Most people, in fact, probably almost all of them, have the ability to train their minds and earn a PhD. Unfortunately, most people also have a lot of other people who will tell them they can't. It's not really the size of the intellect that allows a person to become well educated. It's the size of the drive, dedication, and determination that counts. You don't really get any smarter with an education. You just get more adept at using the intellect God gave you in the first place."

"Well, I don't think I could ever be as smart as you," Brea said.

"Can I tell you a story?"

Brea nodded her assent. Freddie watched, entranced as RJ went on with his story.

"One day, when my son was only seven years old, he said almost the exact same thing to me that you just said. He said he could never be as smart as I am. I told him that a brain was like a glass of water. I'm old, I said. My glass is probably pretty full. You're young, I told him. Your glass is only just starting to fill up. But your glass might be bigger than mine, and we won't know until you get it full. So you need to do your homework and keep up with your studies. Well, that seemed to make him feel a bit better and he walked away. I wasn't really sure that what I said had made my point until about two weeks later when I heard him arguing with his sister. I was just about to step in and stop the argument when I heard him yell, 'Oh yeah! Well, your glass is broken.' I laughed so hard I couldn't go stop the argument. But I knew then that he would be okay. You'll be okay too. Just learn things one at a time and enjoy the ride."

When RJ finished, he glanced up at Freddie. Her eyes were a tiny bit moist. His story wasn't that good, so he wondered if there was a lack of a male role model that he had just accidentally, if momentarily filled. "C'mon," he said, "let's get some ice cream."

While Brea ate her ice cream, Freddie asked RJ if he really believed what he had told Brea or if he was just trying to encourage her.

"I'm not going to tell you that every person on earth has the capacity to earn a doctorate degree, and there are people who are better suited to an advanced degree in one subject over others. What is important is that people know what they can and cannot do and why. Take me for example. I can shoot a bow or a rifle and hit pretty much anything I choose to hit. I am comfortable jumping out of an airplane and going under the sea in a submarine. I can swim forever. I once swam across Santa Rosa Sound up in Pensacola. Did I ever tell you that?"

Without stopping for an answer, he continued, "No, of course not. But with all these things I can do, I cannot play basketball. I cannot dribble or shoot. The reason I tell these stories to people, mostly my students, is that most people are their own biggest impediment to success in life. People stand in the way of their own success through self-doubt, and it is that self-doubt that leads to failure.

"Sure, one needs to prepare before doing hard things. For example, when I made that big swim, I knew I could swim the distance because I did it in a pool first. Then I checked the tides to make sure it was incoming, not outgoing. I didn't want to get swept out to sea. Finally, I arranged for a pickup boat. But I never doubted that I could do it. Making the decision that you can do something, if properly prepared, can set aside the self-doubt and replace it with commitment. It is the commitment that makes it possible. If failure occurs, at least it is a failure like my inability to play basketball. It is a failure resulting from trying, not from being afraid to try."

Freddie asked, "Isn't that a bit arrogant?"

"Actually, no," RJ answered. "Arrogance is an overestimation of one's abilities. What I am talking about is helping people develop a more realistic evaluation of what they can accomplish. I think that because most people underestimate what they can do themselves, then once they meet a person who has an accurate estimate of what can be done, they see him as being arrogant. Back in Texas, there was a pretty common saying: It ain't braggin' if you already done it. It's sort of like that. I think what makes my position much less arrogant is that I find I often believe in what other people can accomplish more than they believe it in themselves. Many of my students have come back and told me that they never thought they could do what they had until I brought it out in them with just such a conversation as we are having now. Frankly, that makes me feel pretty good."

They had been walking as they talked and found themselves at the penguin house. It was odd having penguins in south Florida, but they were still fun to watch. Brea had a wonderful time and imagined, as had probably every other child who had been in the exhibit, what it would be like to be that sleek and agile in the water. Penguins are like the aquatic version of superman. There was a set of twins that RJ and Freddie stood next to as Brea watched the birds. They were arguing about whether sea lions or penguins were better swimmers. The argument was won when the first twin stated flatly that sea lions eat penguins. The victory was short-lived. The other twin pointed out that Orca whales eat sea lions.

RJ laughed a little at that, and Freddie said, "What's so funny?"

"I just get a kick out of what people argue about," RJ said. "And it's not just the kids. Stop in the mall sometime and listen to the arguments people are having as they pass by. It's a riot."

"So," Freddie said, "tell me about these kids you mentioned."

"Well," RJ said, "I have two children from a marriage that I should never have had. But I still am glad I have the kids. Bill, the oldest, is now around thirty. I'm terrible with birthdays and ages. He was born while I was in the service. He's twenty-nine. That's right. My daughter, Megan, is twenty-seven. We are all very close, even though Bill lives in San Diego and Megan is in Lubbock.

That's in Texas. They're great kids." He looked at Freddie and added quite sincerely, "I hope you meet them someday."

Freddie sensed that someday depended on things that had not yet happened, so she smiled and let the subject drop.

28

Saturday at Key Biscayne

The next two weeks passed slowly for Freddie. She wasn't bored by any means. She had her book to write. What made the week drag was that it would be two weeks before she was able to "hang out" with RJ again. He had promised to take her kayaking through the mangrove channels at Key Biscayne Park. RJ spent much of his time with his experiments and his classes. Both Freddie and RJ had spent a lot of their spare time thinking about each other. Finally, Saturday morning came, and just at dawn, RJ pulled into Freddie's drive with his kayak on top of the Land Rover. Freddie had a lunch already packed, and off they went. She had never been on a kayak before and had been nervous. With the help of Google, she had figured out that she needed to be ready to get wet, have a big brimmed hat for the sun, and have water handy. RJ had also provided water, sunscreen, and bug spray, but said they probably would not need the latter.

The kayak design was called a "sit-on-top" kayak. It had been developed specifically for people who were not as adept at using a real kayak and who would most likely use it in the warmer Southern waters. It was really just a big, thick, polypropylene surfboard. It had little depressions in the top where people would sit. There were little cutouts to put your heels into and a cup holder located between the knees of each paddler. The depressions that acted as seats had holes at the bottom to drain out any water that splashed in. Of course that also meant that with each little wave, there was going to be a miniature geyser popping up out of the holes as well. Freddie figured that out and decided to leave her shorts in the car. At RJ's insistence, she kept her shirt on over her bikini to help protect her from the sun. While Freddie was putting her shorts back in the car, RJ began putting sunscreen on his arms and legs. Walking back, Freddie couldn't help notice that he had the strong legs of a swimmer. She liked it. When she got back to the launch ramp, he held up the sunscreen. "Want some?" She did, but she took the tube from his hand to apply it herself while he got the paddles and life preservers.

RJ showed Freddie how to use the double-ended paddle. He then got her situated in the front seat, and they paddled off into the sunrise. The mangrove islands were just waking up as the two paddled into the little channels that separated them. Night Herons glared at them from the lower branches. Great Blue Herons kept a close watch, too, but from their higher roosts. Pelicans sat in their nests or floated on the water but had not begun to feed yet. RJ said that this was because the angle of the sun had to be right in order for the Pelican to be able to see into the water and still not have glare. *Aghh. More physics lessons,* Freddie thought, but then realized that nature was even more fascinating when it was understood better. Nature as a proof of God was more compelling when the complexity and intricacy added a deeper meaning to the more simple visual beauty that surrounded them.

As the sun rose higher, they decided to seek refuge in the shade of a little mangrove channel and have something to eat from Freddie's cooler. The mangrove forests had been chopped up into squares by city and county managers back in the 1930s. These little channels were called mosquito ditches because the idea was to cut the channels to let the swamp drain faster. That way the mosquitoes would have less time to breed. The invention of pesticides had resulted in aerial spraying replacing maintenance of the ditches and most had become overgrown with mangroves creating a tunnel in the forest. A lot of them were too narrow or had filled in with sediment so much that they were not passable, but a good explorer could always find a little hideaway that was wide enough to paddle into. RJ had found just such a place. They followed the channel, which had transformed itself over time to be almost the same as a natural mangrove creek, up under the canopy of mangroves. Along the way, they startled blue crabs in the water and mangrove crabs climbing on the limbs of the trees. They even saw one mangrove water snake curled up in the branches overhead. About a hundred yards up the creek, the channel opened up into a small pond about two hundred feet across. RJ explained that this was probably a place where the original dredge had opened up a place to turn around. Now it was a secluded oasis of natural beauty in the middle of the forest. It was here they stopped for a rest.

They sat quietly and had a snack and a drink. By being quiet, the wildlife eventually determined that the kayakers were not a threat and trees at the edge of the pond slowly became active with a variety of wildlife. Butterflies visited the flowers of the black mangroves. Mangrove Cuckoos chased the butterflies. Night Herons perched just above the water looking for small fish. Snowy egrets waded in the shallow water and a longer-legged American Egret hunted in water that was a little deeper. A large snook cruised slowly through the shallows looking for prey and found it in an unwary shrimp just beneath their kayak.

"This is beautiful," Freddie said. "It's so peaceful. Is this why you brought me here?"

"Freddie," RJ spoke soft and low. "At the end of our hike, I promised to help you get in touch with your spiritual side. The last time I saw you, though, we went to the Seaquarium. I never had the chance then, but I also do not normally forget my promises. Honestly, there is a part of me that tells me that you might like a little more peace in your life. So, yes, I brought you here on purpose and that purpose was for peace."

"Why do you say I need peace? Don't we all need peace?" Freddie inquired.

"I don't know exactly. It's just that sometimes you seem like you have a lot of things bothering you. That's all. If I can help, I will."

Freddie said, "I do have things I need to sort out and actually, I feel very much at ease just being with you. I can't imagine what you would think if you saw me when I was less calm!" She paused. "What do we do now?"

"Come here," RJ said. "Just scoot back in your seat, so that you are leaning up against me." Somehow Freddie managed to move backward without flipping the kayak, and she ended up leaning against RJ's chest. He took her hands in his and folded both their arms across her in a big, loose hug. "We're going to learn to meditate."

RJ paused, and Freddie tried to control her pulse. This was the first time they had been this close, and she found it exciting, uncontrollable, and completely opposite his instructions. She took a couple deep breaths to calm herself. RJ did the same, for he had experienced the same reaction.

"Okay," she said. "I'm ready. What do I do?"

"Close your eyes." RJ's voice was soft and soothing. His lips were just behind Freddie's ear and she could feel his breath on her neck as he spoke. "Make sure you are comfortable. Go ahead and adjust your legs, feet, and arms so that there are no sharp or distracting pressure points." Freddie wriggled a bit and then settled into his arms again.

RJ spoke slowly into Freddie's ear. "Good. Now let your mind become receptive. Don't think of things. Don't focus on anything. But don't stifle your thoughts either. Let them come to you. Just be passive. As each thought comes, acknowledge it. Accept it. You will probably think of mundane things first, like needing to do the laundry when you get home or what you need at the grocery store. When each of these thoughts arise, by accepting them, you can also put them aside. They will come back later when you can do something about them. Soon, more meaningful thoughts will arise. With each of these, as before, you can acknowledge them, accept them, and own the responsibility to act on them while also putting them aside because out here in this mangrove pool there is nothing to actually do about any of them."

Freddie nodded ever so slightly. For the next few minutes, RJ said nothing at all. He could feel Freddie's muscles relaxing. He could sense her breathing and her heart rate, both of which were slowing down. She was just barely awake and facing each of her thoughts and problems as they arose. He could tell she was being successful by how calm she felt. Finally, he whispered in her ear. "You will probably find that there is one thought that keeps coming back even though you have tried to set it aside." Freddie's head nodded ever so slightly. "This is the one you will now let stay. No longer put it aside. Look at this thought and ask it to answer itself." RJ felt the slightest tension in Freddie's neck, so he continued. "Don't force it. Just give your problem time to explain itself." Freddie relaxed again. "Every problem has an answer. They come as a set. When our logical mind can't solve the problem, it is because we are not letting our spirit speak to us loudly enough. In this answer, we may find a path that is completely hidden from our conscious mind, yet it may well be the best path for us to take."

Again, RJ could feel the slightest nod of Freddie's head against his cheek. "I think you may have done this with the thought you had that kept coming back so can I go on?" Freddie nodded again, almost imperceptibly. "Now that this thought is paired with a possible solution, it will allow you to put it aside." Freddie nodded again. "Now your mind is clear, and you will find yourself face-to-face with that side of you that we call our spirit. You have always known her. She has always been there. She is inspiration. She is sudden insight. She is hope. Sometimes she is a dream. Once you find her, you will find that through her you can reach the spirits of others."

As RJ whispered these words, Freddie felt that tingle one gets when a foot has fallen asleep. It began in her hands, which RJ still held clasped over her stomach. It traveled into her where her hands touched her skin and filled her chest and her heart. At some point, she felt the same energy coming from RJ's heart enter her through her back where the two bodies were closest together. In an instant, it was there and then gone. She wondered if it had been real. She wondered if the new understanding she had of herself and of RJ had been real or if she had fallen into a dream state. She wondered if her new and even more comfortable feeling about their relationship was real or imagined. She wondered only until he whispered, "Did you feel that?"

Freddie nodded again, so very quietly. RJ let her enjoy the moment for a minute or two more and then pulled his hands from hers and brought them up her arms to her shoulders. "It's time to go now."

The trip back to the launch was pretty quiet. RJ knew that Freddie had a lot to think about, and Freddie knew that even though there was a deeper and very close connection between them, she was unable to talk about it. RJ dropped her off at home with the usual exchanges of chitchat. Yes, they both had a good time. The lunch was great. Wasn't it wonderful that the mosquitoes hadn't been out. The sad part, for RJ, was that he still saw that Freddie was holding back. Nonetheless, as he walked her to her door, he suggested that the next time they saw each other, they should do something more conventional, like see a movie. Freddie agreed and went inside, the calmness still permeating every part of her body and soul.

The rest of the day and into the night, Freddie tried to figure out her day. The meditation technique that RJ had shown her was similar to things she had read about in self-help books. She thought she had tried them according to the instructions, but now she knew that she had failed to reach the state that she had with RJ's help. That part she could accept. The whole tingly sensation, though, was just too much. She had to admit that she felt it, and she even marveled at the implication that RJ had felt it too. She still questioned if it was real. It could have been nothing more than one of those unpredictable shivers that run through people from time to time. Maybe RJ had felt her muscles twitch, and he was asking if she felt it too. Later that night, she tried it again with a fair amount of success. When she got herself situated and began to put her troubles and thoughts aside, she was left staring her own soul in the face. She was telling herself that she did have a soul and that her spirit was good and pure and eager to help her find her way. Her spirit was telling her that she was falling in love with RJ. She was not ready to deal with that, even though, as RJ had said, problems and solutions came in sets.

29

Thursday

All the next week, Freddie either worked on her book or looked for places to submit her resume. She had given it to a placement service but was continuing to look on her own as well. It was a productive week for both efforts.

Her first success came at the end of three long days of writing her manuscript. One of the things that had eluded her had been her title, and the little blurb she was supposed to write as a summary. Her professor had called it an abstract. Once she had completed almost all of the profiles, though, she had put RJ's method to the test. She calmed herself and put all her other distractions aside. And there it was. She opened her eyes and typed:

Psychological Profiles of Twenty-Five Male Clients of a South Florida Dating Service. A thesis in partial fulfillment of a Master of Science Degree in the field of Psychology by Winifred Beatrice Kazlowski.

ABSTRACT: In this work, the principal researcher used immersion and observation techniques to interview twenty-five males who were clients of a dating service. The selection of the test subjects was partially randomized by setting parameters, which the agent for the service was required to use in selecting potential introductions. The researcher met each person a minimum of three times. Subjects were not aware that the author was conducting psychological research. Male subjects were between the ages of thirty and fifty years of age and were required to be single or divorced, not in the process of getting a divorce, and must not have criminal records. Profiles were generated based on interviews and the information that the agency was legally allowed to share. The agency was not informed of the research in order to avoid introducing a bias into the selection of subjects. Profiles were clustered into psychological groupings, and statistical frequency analysis was conducted to produce profiles, which were most and least likely to be encountered. In the interest of privacy, the names, places, times, and calendar dates of the interviews conducted under the guise of arranged dates have been changed in this paper.

Freddie had stopped typing, failing to complete the abstract. It would be normal to include a summary of her overall findings in the abstract, but she wanted to do two things first. She needed to talk to her advisor and she needed to finish one last profile: Randall J. Hunter.

30

The Job Interview

Her second success came Friday morning. She had received a call from the placement service, and she had a job interview with a defense contractor, Intellispace Avionics. This was familiar territory for her, and her only concern had been that the engineering firm might be one that Noah and she had done business with in the past. There were problems in that scenario that she didn't even want to begin to face. She decided to go to the interview in what she called her "business hot" outfit. It was, for all practical purposes, a business pants suit. But the fitted white shirt, small red neckerchief, covered by a short gray jacket, which was just short enough to let her show off her ass added the hot part. Long legs with a medium pair of heels made her taller, without being imposing. She was fully prepared to make a physical impression followed by a killer interview in which she would demonstrate her mental prowess and what really was an in-depth understanding of the business. She would not have to fake anything. Her confidence was shattered when she was shown into the office for her interview. There, in front of her, was Spencer Ford.

Somehow, she managed to conceal her shock. She hadn't even thought of Spencer since the day she made up that appointment with him for cover so she could rush home and get rid of Richard's bouquet. Spencer was a tall, dark-haired, and very intelligent engineer. She and he had known each other for years. It was plain to see, however, that today he was seeing her in a whole new light. He took in her figure and her attitude in one quick but appreciative glance and offered his hand.

"You look well, Freddie." He smiled. "How have you been?"

Freddie regained her balance. "Forget about me, how have you been? In fact, what are you doing here? I thought you were on the fast track to being a part owner at Pierce-Evans Hydraulics."

Freddie had deftly turned the conversation back to Spencer pretty quickly. She needed time to think. Would doing business with Spencer be okay or not okay? He was the same guy she knew before, but the company was one she and Noah had never dealt with or even worked together with on any proposals.

Spencer answered politely. "I was. But I was always on the track to part ownership, not full ownership. Intellispace, as it turns out, was in a bit of a bind. The principal, Jason Fowler, is a nice guy, but he had come from a very small family. He'd never married. He'd outlived all his cousins and other relatives and had no one to leave the company to when he was gone. He was adamant that IA would never go public. Apparently, he felt rather strongly that when a company went public, the owners would all be strangers. They would be shareholders interested in the margin more than the product. This happens in business all the time actually. He had decided that he didn't want a legacy of profit margin—he wanted a legacy of engineering excellence and quality manufacturing. When we met, he was apparently not only impressed with my skills but also with the fact that we shared a desire to achieve and maintain the best. He was already a millionaire, so he decided to retire, and he sold me fifty-one percent of the stock on the condition that as long as I lived I would maintain the tradition that he and I had just created. When it was my time, I would find another Spencer Ford to take my place.

"The other forty-nine percent of the stock was transferred to the employees equally. Every person who works here has an equal share in the corporation. If they leave, for whatever reason, the shares are returned to the corporation under a buy-back agreement. If a new person is hired, they are issued equal shares. I'm in charge, but we all benefit. The staff finds it very motivating."

During his explanation, Freddie had taken a seat in the interview chair, and Spencer had seated himself behind the desk. Without missing a beat, she had noticed that he had noticed the way she had crossed her legs. It was apparent that he was physically attracted to her. It was fortunate that she was quite used to that. She realized that while she had not known her interviewer, he had certainly known who was being interviewed. What piqued her interest was whether it was the physical attraction or her intellectual skills that had landed her the interview in the first place. Her uncertainty was short-lived. After about fifteen minutes of what amounted to friendly chitchat, Spencer got to the heart of the matter. She actually had noticed that about him before: He liked to get things done without a lot of posturing and fanfare.

"I've been reviewing your application, and quite honestly I was surprised at first. Our interactions before had been limited to what you let me see: a receptionist. Since this landed on my desk from the agency, however, I've been doing a little checking. I contacted the advertising agencies you worked with in your former position. I contacted the web design company. I even contacted a couple of your co-workers. To put you at ease, I did not contact Noah. I should have mentioned it before that I knew about you and he being divorced, but one never knows whether to offer condolences or congratulations." He smiled inquisitively, and Freddie laughed, putting him at ease.

"Let's say it was mutual," Freddie said. "But I am glad you did not ask him for a reference."

"Good. Now that I have a full understanding of what you actually did for Noah's company and I see that you not only have a university degree but will soon receive a master's of science in psychology...oh, yes. I checked with the university on that. Anyway, now that I have a complete understanding of your skills, I am prepared to offer you the position of vice president. We don't even need to go through the mundane interviewing protocol. I see what you did for Noah, and I want you to do it for IA. No job description, just like it says on your resume. You will be responsible for managing the corporate profile from top to bottom."

Freddie was actually quite taken aback by the offer and told Spencer that she would have to think it over. Spencer said he would have expected nothing less. They didn't talk at all about salary or how many shares she would get as a new employee. At this level, people decide to work together and then work out the details. If the details are what will make the partnership work, then it will never work.

She would get to that decision next week. It was Friday night and she had a date with RJ.

31

RJ's Distraction

RJ had spent most of the week trying to make sense out of the data from the sound experiment with the fishing net. The data was good. The sound receivers recorded directional and amplitude shifts in the compression waves. He thought about conducting a follow-up experiment in the wave tank in the lab, but the walls of the tank would foul things up. Any sound wave would encounter that hard wall and reflect back into the tank where it would mix in with the experimental waves. The problem was that even at a microscale, he couldn't get the mathematics precise enough to recreate the observed data. Finally he came to the only conclusion possible. He just didn't know enough. His experiment was spur of the moment and not thought out ahead of time. As a result, the design was too complex. No, he corrected himself. It was too simplistic. He thought he could get what he needed easily, but reality was more complex than he had anticipated. *Sort of like my relationship with Freddie*, he mused to himself.

In his net experiment, he had small string diameter and the lines didn't go up and down. They went on a slant. Adding to the problems, the mesh of the net was not tight, and so each little diamond it made was actually a different size and shape. He still thought the theory was good, but he needed a fixed frame, not a loose net, and he needed to precalculate the wave interference patterns so that he could select a string diameter and mesh size that would maximize his ability to detect the interference patterns in the waves. The reason he stayed intrigued was because if he could figure out the basics, he could add complexity later, and then perhaps create a sound mask for submarines and other underwater sounds. One benefit was that a netted sound mask would be porous enough that water could flow through it. That might also eliminate some other problems he was having with his research. Just like with Freddie, he thought, *If he could get the basics down…*

RJ stopped himself again. It seemed like every thought he had somehow ran itself back to Freddie. If it weren't for that pesky feeling that she was being a little less than completely honest, he could see this going somewhere really pleasant. Somehow, and he couldn't yet see how, it all seemed to stem from this book that she said no one would read. Freddie seemed open to talk about almost anything else except how well she was doing with her classes and that book. RJ consoled himself by telling himself that she would share when the time came, and if it never came then they weren't right for each other anyway.

32

You

By Friday afternoon, RJ had become rather comfortable with Freddie as a friend who might eventually grow into something more. All that stood in the way was her reticence to share everything. Freddie, on the other hand was having very strong emotional feelings for RJ. While she already accepted him as a friend, it was his potential as a lover that dominated her thoughts. She didn't realize that it was her own inability to share her project with him that stood in the way of her seeing them in a fully developed friendship. Still, even if there were still some things to get through, the level of just being comfortable with each other surpassed anything either one had felt with anyone else in their entire lives.

The evening went well. How could it be otherwise? Dinner was filled with casual conversation. Freddie brought him up to date on Brea's latest school projects, and RJ vented his frustration over his experiment. RJ shared some challenges he was having with a particular but nameless graduate student, and Freddie shared with him her new job offer. Of course she left out the details about the role that her new degree played, but she did thank him for his help with putting her experience in a more appropriate light. She said it had helped immensely.

The movie was nothing special, but it was accented with all the things that normally happen in movies. There was whispering, which brought their faces close together and caused their hearts to beat a little faster. There was elbow bumping, which eventually turned into interlocked arms because it was simply a more comfortable way to sit. There was also the occasional hand on the other one's knee or thigh when the appropriate scene in the movie called for it. As they walked to the car, neither one wanted the evening to actually end. Freddie's hand found its way into RJ's as they walked. He took it without hesitation, and they gave each other a smile. It was that soft, smile of simply being content with each other.

RJ held the door for Freddie and walked around to the other side of the jeep to get in. As he started the engine, he looked over at her and, thinking she might want a drink, said, "It's still a bit early. What do you want to do now?"

Freddie put her hand to his face, looked him in the eyes, and said, "You." Then she kissed him. It was not a hard or passionate kiss. It was gentle and almost wispy the way her lips fluttered against his. He couldn't tell that she was terrified that he would say he wasn't ready yet.

RJ was quiet for a long time as he drove Freddie home. He hadn't expected this and was not sure exactly what to make of it. He decided to let it ride on whatever happened when he walked her to her door. Freddie's mind was at peace with her offer and with his silence. She had received her final divorce papers from Jennifer in the mail the day before. For some reason, it had been important to her that she waited for it. Maybe it was RJ's spiritual connection. It didn't matter how or why. What mattered was that it was now okay. What mattered was that he was ready too.

He pulled into the drive and got out to get her door. He took her hand in his as they walked to the door. They turned to look at each other. Under the porch light, she looked almost like an angel to him. RJ put his hands on her waist and drew her to him. This would be their first good-night kiss, even if it was their second kiss. He could feel her heart race as their lips met. Freddie's arms went up around his neck. A few, long seconds later, she pulled back an inch, looked into his eyes, and said, "Come inside."

33

Saturday Morning

RJ opened his eyes. The morning light was coming softly in through the sheer curtains. On the pillow next to him was Freddie's still sleeping face. She was as beautiful in sleep as she was when she was awake. This thought actually made him chuckle a little as he thought, "At least she isn't a pillow drooler."

His slight laugh woke her, and she opened her eyes. Looking straight into his, she said, "Thank you."

"For what?" RJ asked.

"For not rushing me. It seems like everyone I have met since I got divorced just wanted an easy piece. When I met you, it seemed like you wanted me for me. It was like I meant something as a person. My ex-husband treated my body like a playpen, and I was so dumb I didn't even realize it. It has been nice to meet someone who can see my mind and my soul. For one thing, it has assured me that I still have one."

Her confession lit the fire again, and it was another thirty minutes before they managed to actually get out of bed and start the coffeepot. In Freddie's kitchen, at the same table where Brea did her homework, the breakfast conversation was light. There was one thing that had bothered Freddie, however, and this seemed like a good time to ask about it.

"RJ?" she asked. "I want to know something, if it isn't too personal."

RJ laughed. "There isn't much that gets more personal than our last twelve hours, so go ahead. Shoot."

"Oh, stop it. But really. You are a really smart man and you could work for anyone you wanted. In the private sector, you could pull down an easy three to four hundred thousand dollars a year doing exactly the same thing you do at the university for less than a hundred thousand. Don't you want to be successful?"

RJ sipped at his coffee and examined Freddie's face. Maybe this was the part he was missing. Maybe this was the part she was missing in him. Either way, it was the part that was going to be coming out. He wondered if it had anything to do with that book that no one would read.

"How do you know how much I earn?" he finally said.

She blushed a bit and thought about saying it was a guess but decided to tell the truth. "I looked up the standard pay scale at the university and figured out where you were likely to be, and then I Googled up the latest contract the university has with the Defense Department and found what was listed as your overhead. Was that bad?"

RJ laughed. "No. It wasn't bad. In fact it was resourceful. But it was also quite unnecessary. I would have told you if you had just asked. But to answer your question, Yes. Of course I want to be successful. But I suspect I might see success in a different way than many people. How do you define being successful, Freddie?"

Freddie was now on the spot. "I suppose I mean what most people mean. Being successful means having a nice house, going on nice vacations, being able to support your family comfortably, not worrying about your next paycheck, and I guess being able to retire comfortably when the time comes."

"Right," RJ said. "That would be the way most people define it. For myself, I define success as having built the person that I am comfortable dying as. The amount of money I make at the university isn't the most money I could make. It might, however, be the most money I can make and still be the person I like to be. It most certainly is enough to buy everything I need, if not everything to satisfy every whim I might have. I have a very comfortable place to live. My vacations come every summer even if they are wrapped into a research cruise. I am perfectly happy with my situation and having a bigger paycheck wouldn't change that."

RJ put his hand on Freddie's and held it while he gazed into her eyes with sincerity. "What would change is that I would be working at the bidding of others. At the university, I am required to get grants and work on things, but they are the ones I want to work on and not the things I must work on because the boss signed a contract with someone. We've all heard the saying that you can't take it with you. As a youngster, I realized that the only things you can take with you are your character and personality. These are the things your soul is made of. These are my treasures. So I consider myself to be quite successful even if I can't decide right now to go get in my private jet and fly you to Paris for lunch."

RJ had delivered this explanation in such kind and gentle manner that it didn't come across as a criticism for how she had defined success. It was just a statement about the fact that he was happy with his choices and had no regrets. Then he added.

"The only thing missing in my achieving my own definition of success is that I have not found someone to share it."

Freddie kissed him softly and thanked him with all the sincerity in her heart for being so honest.

An hour later, RJ had gone off to tend to an experiment that his students were conducting in the lab. Yes, it was Saturday, he admitted, but students often found the weekends to be good times to run experiments because there were no classes, and they could run for a long time. Brea had come home from Sarah's and shortly afterward had headed out into the yard. Freddie sat quietly in her kitchen and reflected on her situation. She had just had a marvelous night of physical enjoyment and spiritual sharing. She thought she was in love. She also thought that she may never be able to achieve RJ's level of—she struggled for the word and finally settled on "complacency."

She may never be complacent with just having enough to be comfortable. Her years with Noah in the big house with the Porsche and the wonderful clothes and vacations to exotic places had become an elixir she may not be able to put down. She knew Noah had used her as window dressing for his business and for his nightly pleasures, but she was also coming to realize that the price may have been right for what she had received in terms of the ease of her lifestyle. These thoughts didn't change how she felt about not being recognized for what she had done. That price was too high. The question was whether she could give it up. *Hell*, she thought. She didn't even know if she was going to have to give it up. With the job offer from Spencer, she could eventually earn more than Noah. But she thought the job was based on her earning her degree. With that thought, she redoubled her resolve to finish quickly.

Just then the phone rang. "Hello, this is Freddie."

"Hi, Freddie. Spencer here. I hope I am not calling too early on a Saturday."

"No. It's fine. What's up?"

"Well, I am about to throw a wrench into everything we talked about last week."

"Oh no," Freddie said. "What's going on?"

"Well, I need to ask you a question, but before I do, I need to make sure that you know that no matter what you say, the job offer is still yours to take if you decide you want it. I'm a grownup, and I can easily separate out my personal and private life from my professional one and I hope you can as well."

"Okay," Freddie said. "I think I can handle that." To herself, she wondered where the hell this was going.

"Freddie, I always thought you were someone special even if I didn't know how much you contributed to Noah's company. I have to admit that I was attracted to you the moment I saw you four years ago. I confess that there have been times when I made appointments with Noah when I could have handled the matter with a phone call just so I could have a conversation with you while I waited. I know that under other circumstances these actions would sound like stalking, but as I said, I was able to keep things separate. When I saw you again the other day, I realized you were no longer Noah's wife and receptionist, but you were the most beautiful woman I have ever had the pleasure of knowing. I decided that risking losing you as a business partner was worth the possibility of gaining your company as my date, if even for one night. You can have both. You can have neither. Or as I said, you can still have the job and I will go on about my life. You are a beautiful and talented woman and I would like to take you out for an evening of unabashed courtship."

"Oh, wow, Spencer. Now I have two things to think about. Both of them are quite nice and quite appealing. I promise I will let you know on both accounts by next weekend."

34

Writer's Block

That afternoon, Freddie was faced with yet another challenge. It was time to write RJ's profile.

Freddie began and tore up at least twenty paragraphs on RJ. The only consistent thing in each of them was that he was the only one of the twenty-five men who was not on the prowl for the first opportunity to get laid. He genuinely wanted to find a companion first and a lover second. RJ had shared how he had lived his life, and it was unusual. He had been fortunate to find his spiritual side as a young man. He was still in his teens when his own personal epiphany had put him in touch with both himself and with his God. He had not shared the details of these events, but the fact was that once he had found God he was able to find his soul, his spirit. He was able to differentiate his spirit from his conscious being. When he later read Freud's description of the id, ego, and superego, he easily identified with all three. What Freud had missed was due to his atheism. Freud failed to recognize the soul in the triad, which he so clearly wrote about as a treatise in psychology. As RJ grew and made life choices, he was able to tap into his own spirit and subsequently into that spirit, which his grandmother had often referred to as his guardian angel. He felt a companionship with his guardian angel and more. He felt it with other angels that his spirit had told him were out there. He even gave them names. Eventually, he also felt close to his favorite saints. When faced with his difficult choices, he would often meditate on his choice and his most appropriate saint. The proper choice for him always came as what others might describe as a gut feeling. His faith let him follow it, and his choices were always better than the ones that his intellect had selected for him. Freddie remembered that as a young girl, the Catholic nuns had told her this was prayer. RJ just seemed to explain it better.

RJ had shared all of this as well as the fact that his technique seldom worked when it came to choosing female companionship. It was not until much later in life that he had learned to go beyond simply making a spiritual connection with a woman and being able to determine her spiritual character. Because of this failing, he had been hurt many times. It was because of this that she couldn't just leave him out. She would stop short of writing that she believed all of this, but she could not contradict the fact that this was how RJ perceived himself. His profile was both unique and critical to her research being complete. RJ had taught her that a scientist doesn't just throw out data because it isn't what was expected. The scientist needed to adjust to the data, not adjust the data itself.

Each of the profiles on RJ, which she started to write gradually, fell apart into nothing less than a love sonnet. They could have been written by any high school girl with a crush on the quarterback. Her professor would never go for that. Finally she decided that she needed to talk with her and get her advice.

Freddie called the office of Dr. Jessica Garner and left a voicemail that she was having trouble with a particular passage of her thesis. She asked for an appointment for Wednesday and then sent a follow-up e-mail with the same information and request. She also sent in a copy of the draft thesis, which she had prepared up to that point.

35

The End of the World

Wednesday was the end of Freddie's world. At least it was the end of the one she had been building for the past two months. Dr. Garner had read her draft and had found it fascinating. Of course there were rough spots, but those could easily be ironed out. She also shared the fact that she had given Freddie a recommendation to an engineering company and had assured them that Freddie was well on the way to receiving her degree. Dr. Garner saw nothing that stood in her way. When they got into the topic of Freddie's mental block, Freddie felt that she had to tell Dr. Garner everything in order to get the right advice. She confessed to dating RJ but made certain to point out that the three dates that she had kept for interviews had been completed before they started seeing each other. She even confessed to sleeping with him and to having entertained the notion that she was in love with him.

Dr. Garner had grown quite serious as Freddie's story unfolded. Dating a subject during the course of her research was a clear violation of scientific protocols. Completing the three interviews before she had become intimate with the subject made no difference to her at all. The fact that she had slept with him only made it worse. Dr. Garner asked how she could possibly provide an unbiased profile under these circumstances. Freddie admitted that this was in fact her exact problem. She was unable to sort out the RJ she knew from the RJ she would have profiled based only on the three interviews.

Dr. Garner saw only one way out that would preserve her degree. Of course, she did offer that Freddie could simply drop out and not get her degree, but neither of them liked that prospect. Faculty who had students drop out did not have as high of a standing as those who cranked out student after student. So far, Garner had a perfect record and was not going to spoil it because Freddie couldn't keep her pants on. She was so disappointed in Freddie that she actually told her as much. She did let Freddie know that she would never recommend her for a license to practice therapy, but if she promised to limit the use of her education to applied marketing principles, there was a way to still get her degree.

Freddie listened intently and with tears in her eyes as Dr. Garner explained. Freddie would give her notes and recordings of the three interviews with RJ to Dr. Garner. Garner herself would write up the last profile, but Freddie would still need to write the analysis and interpretation section of her thesis. Freddie would need to stop seeing RJ. There could be no more dating. None. If Garner ever found out that it had continued, she assured Freddie that she had the power to strip her of her degree. Dr. Garner emphasized this brutally. Freddie would not be allowed to see RJ socially ever again, and if she did, Dr. Garner assured her that she would file a complaint, which would cause the university to revoke the award. Freddie didn't know that this was an empty threat and that Garner had no such power but did not realize it until much later. Dr. Garner gave Freddie until Monday to think it over and asked her to leave her office.

When Freddie got home, she cried until it was time to go get Brea from school. She cleaned herself up and went off to get her. On the way, she tried to think of what she could do. As it turned out, her best option was to talk it over with Spencer. How did she know? It was in her gut. She couldn't say why really. The feeling was just there, and it was strong. She sent Spencer a text message that she would see him Saturday night at the Banana Boat lounge. It was a quiet little bar with a deck out over the water. She realized to her amazement that it was the time crunch of having to pick up Brea that had heightened her awareness to the point of making her choice. She hadn't thought this through at all. She had felt it through. Maybe she had learned a little something from RJ after all.

36

Saturday

By Saturday night, Freddie had regained some sense of composure. She had spent an hour every morning and another hour every night meditating the way RJ had shown her. Counting Wednesday night and Saturday morning, this had given her six hours to meditate on herself and her situation. She thought about what RJ had said: "Success is building the person you are happy to die as." She thought about Brea. She thought about the new job offer. Most of all, she thought about how and where she fit into these other thoughts. There had also been several rather pleasant phone calls with RJ. The conversations were casual, and they did not explore their relationship beyond the point of friends who have slept together. They both knew that they wanted to see each other again. They both knew that they wanted each other again. And neither knew if that would actually come to pass. The only tense moment was when RJ asked how the book was coming. Freddie wanted to tell him the truth about it but couldn't. Her degree and her future meant too much. She kept telling herself *Maybe later* even though she knew that later might never come.

Whether these thoughts made sense to her by Saturday night or whether she was just learning to live with them was not clear even to Freddie. What was clear was that she needed to bury them when Spencer picked her up.

Her date with Spencer went exactly the way she had hoped. He was a perfect gentleman. He was very frank about how beautiful she was and also very frank about how much he wanted her as a business partner even if she didn't find him attractive at all. He did take special pains in reminding her of all the little things he had done over the years. There were flowers on her birthday, chocolate at Christmas, and through the course of everything, she did remember him coming into the office twenty minutes early for a meeting. She remembered that he had always been pleasant and never inappropriate. With his prior confession, she was able to see that these were the acts of a man stifling his attraction.

Spencer assured her that whatever choice she made, he would do everything in his power to make it be the right choice. He comforted her with the knowledge that he had suppressed his attraction to her for years before, and he could certainly do it again if he had to. He was also quick to add that he didn't want to. Neither did he promise that an excursion into a dating relationship would lead to anything substantial. He was again quick to add that the only way to find out was to try it. Freddie thought to herself that in many ways, he was a lot like RJ in this regard.

37

Finding Freddie

On Sunday morning, Freddie went again into her thoughts to try and sort them out. Spencer was a good man. He was every bit as intelligent as RJ and every bit the gentleman. He cared about Brea, just like RJ did. Sitting at the kitchen table with her coffee, meditating on these thoughts, she found herself with RJ, Spencer, and Brea—or at least she was dreaming about being with them. Maybe she was actually interacting with their spirits. It didn't really matter. RJ told her that he was happy with who he is. Freddie said she was happy with who he is too, but did her spirit and RJ's match? RJ had told her that the connection alone was not enough. There had to be an interlacing of spirits. Was that what she felt when she just felt comfortable with him? What about Brea? Would RJ's attitude about success provide her what she needed to attend a first rate college? Would her desire to excel at IA with Spencer become a sore spot with RJ? Would he find her desire to achieve material wealth unattractive? Could she, or even should she, suppress her desire for material wealth? RJ's spirit told her that she would be equally attractive either way. RJ's spirit asked her if her drive to achieve these things would lead to her not having respect for him? Could she be happy with his lesser needs? Was she being selfish by wanting her degree? Was she being selfish by wanting a good and secure future for Brea? Was she putting her needs ahead of Brea's? Or was she putting Brea's needs ahead of her own?

When Freddie arrived at this question, clarity came up from the pool of confusion like a whale surfacing at sea. Could it be that the truly selfish choice was to choose love over security and practicality? It seemed as though it might when the losses were to be shared by Brea. She could not be certain about her relationship with either RJ or Spencer. With her degree in her hand, she would not need to rely on others. She asked if placing her degree over love was an act of selfishness or an act of love for her daughter that would assure her daughter's future no matter how her own relationships fared. With her degree, she would be able to rely on herself for the things she had previously received from Noah.

Spencer's spirit moved in and out of these thoughts. Spencer was not in conflict with her goals. Spencer was actually helping her to achieve her goals. The problem was that she didn't love Spencer. At least, not yet. She loved RJ, or thought she did. But it was RJ who had taught her to follow her own spirit. It was RJ who taught her that problems came with solutions. It was RJ who gave her the answer she sought even if it wasn't the answer she had wanted to find.

38

Monday

Monday morning, Freddie knocked on Dr. Garner's door, opened it, and dropped the recordings of her dates with RJ and her draft manuscript on her desk. "There's my decision," she said and she left.

Ending things with RJ was impossible to do on the phone. She invited him over, with every intention of telling him everything. When he came in, he took her in his arms and kissed her. She turned her cheek to him instead of kissing him back. He looked at her and asked, "What's the matter?"

Freddie looked up into RJ's eyes as her own filled with tears. Her body shook as he held her gently in his arms. One last time, Freddie failed to find the strength. "I can't tell you. I'm sorry. I don't want to hurt you."

Freddie left the room in tears, and RJ closed the door gently as he left.

In his gut, in his soul, he knew that this was the best ending because it was the ending her spirit had chosen. Even so, he joined up on a two-month research cruise and left the next week. He needed the time.

About eight months later, RJ read in the paper that Winifred Kazlowski, M.S., had married Spencer Ford. He was happy for Freddie. The initials after her name confirmed his suspicions about that book that no one would ever read. It was her thesis. He wanted to go to the university library and read that book, but he never did.